Clubbing Forever

Clubbing
Forever

Helena Pielichaty

Illustrated by Melanie Williamson

OXFORD
UNIVERSITY PRESS

OXFORD
UNIVERSITY PRESS

Great Clarendon Street, Oxford OX2 6DP

Oxford University Press is a department of the University of Oxford.
It furthers the University's objective of excellence in research, scholarship,
and education by publishing worldwide in

Oxford New York

Auckland Cape Town Dar es Salaam Hong Kong Karachi
Kuala Lumpur Madrid Melbourne Mexico City Nairobi
New Delhi Shanghai Taipei Toronto

With offices in

Argentina Austria Brazil Chile Czech Republic France Greece
Guatemala Hungary Italy Japan Poland Portugal Singapore
South Korea Switzerland Thailand Turkey Ukraine Vietnam

Oxford is a registered trade mark of Oxford University Press
in the UK and in certain other countries

British Library Cataloguing in Publication Data

Data available

ISBN: 978-0-19-275533-9

3 5 7 9 10 8 6 4 2

Typset by Palimpsest Book Production Limited, Polmont, Stirlingshire
Printed in Great Britain by Cox & Wyman Ltd, Reading, Berkshire

Alex's Back

for Oliver James and Lucy Isobel

Jolene's Back

Dedicated to:

Bretton Hall College, Wakefield
1948–2007
. . . especially those trained as teachers
during the vintage years
1974–1978

Contents

Alex's Back

—the girl who's trying to keep life simple (but simply can't do it)

Chapter One

This New Year just gone—it's May now so we're talking five months ago—I couldn't think of one single New Year resolution to make. My mum's was to learn how to use the computer properly. My big sister Caitlin's was to revise every night for her A levels and to pass her driving test, and my dead brother Daniel's was to get a tattoo. Dad's was to stop coating his food in salt but I was stuck when it came to thinking of one for myself. I couldn't think of *anything*. In the end, I asked my dad to think of one for me, seeing as I'd thought of his. Dad put down his cup of tea, stretched out his legs in front of the fire, and had a ponder. 'Keep life simple, Alex. If you do that, you won't go far wrong,' he said.

'OK, then, my New Year resolution is to keep life simple,' I announced, thinking what a doddle it was compared to Caitlin's.

I got going on it straight away. The two biggest pains in my life were deciding what to wear and worrying about friendship groups, so I decided only to wear black clothes, apart from school uniform, and only to have one best friend, Jolene Nevin. The last one was perfect because Jolene lived miles and miles away and I only heard from her by e-mail. My life couldn't have been simpler, even if I lived on a desert island in the middle of an ocean with nothing but coconuts for company. Sorted.

That's what I thought, anyway, until May. May was when my New Year resolution bit the dust. Unlike when Caitlin failed her driving test by reversing into a bottle bank  last month, I didn't know immediately that my reso-

lution was doomed. It kind of crept up on me slowly, like my grandma once told me rheumatism does.

It was last lesson on a Wednesday afternoon, choir practice in the hall with Mr Sharkey, the headteacher at my school, Zetland Avenue Primary, when the creeping-up business started. Mr Sharkey was in one of his Sarky Sharkey moods. He doesn't get them often, but when he does, we all know about it.

We had just finished the last verse of 'One more Step' when he turned away from us and began bowing so dramatically in front of Mrs Pisarski at the piano his springy beard almost touched the parquet floor. 'That was fantastic, Mrs Pisarski! Fantastic! I heard every note as clear as anything. We were all lost for words at your magnificence!'

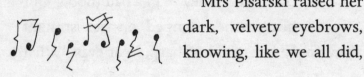 Mrs Pisarski raised her dark, velvety eyebrows, knowing, like we all did,

5

that Mr Sharkey wasn't paying her a compliment so much as insulting us. 'OK,' Mr Sharkey continued, loosening his tie and turning to the middle of the hall where we were standing in three rows of eight. He was ready to get down to the nitty-gritty. 'Now, if you'd all care to join in this time . . .'

'As if we didn't just then!' Sammie Wesley moaned out loud from beside me. Sammie's a year above me—a Year Six—but we hang out in choir because we go to After School club together afterwards.

Mr Sharkey immediately cupped his hand behind his ear. 'What's that? Did someone speak?' he asked gruffly.

'Yes; it was me, a little mouse from Fairyland,' Sammie whispered in a silly squeak that sounded nothing like.

Big mistake. Everyone knows headteachers have abnormal powers of hearing, especially when they're in a bad mood. Our headteacher jumped on her straight away, fixing her with his sharp, clear eyes. 'What was that, Miss Wesley? You want to sing a solo? Absolutely. Out you come.'

'Not likely!' Sammie protested, pulling her fizzy strawberry-blonde hair in front of her face in a feeble effort to hide herself. She's quite shy, really, for a noisy person.

Instead of forcing her to step forward, which he might have done if he'd been in a really, really bad mood, Mr Sharkey let out a huge sigh and looked deflated. 'Listen, folks,' he said tiredly, his eyes roaming across the three rows so we knew he meant *everyone*, 'you all know that last effort was pathetic; a constipated pigeon could have made more noise! "With a spring" it instructs at the beginning: "a *spring*". You lot couldn't spring if I put you on a trampoline built on a mile-high stack of giant mattresses.'

Everyone slumped their shoulders and began muttering mutinously but I knew exactly what he meant because I love singing too and we *had* been pathetic. Maybe he could sense my sympathetic aura because just then he fixed his eyes straight at me.

'Alex . . .'

Oh no. I glanced at the clock; only five minutes left until the end of school. Parents were already peering through the hall windows as they waited for their kids. My heart sank and I exchanged looks with Sammie. This half-term's topic at After School club was 'Food Glorious Food' and tonight we were making the best meal in the world—pizzas. If we didn't get over there on the dot all the best toppings would go.

'Alex,' Mr Sharkey repeated.

'Do I have to?' I asked him.

'Yep.'

'But why?'

Mr Sharkey flung his arm dramatically across his forehead, pretending to be shocked, which meant he was perking up a bit. 'Why? Why, she asks? Did Jonny Wilkinson ask his PE teacher "why?" when he was picked for the rugby team? Did Leonardo da Vinci shake his head and say "why?" when someone gave him canvas and charcoal?

Did Aretha Franklin ask "why?" when she picked up a microphone? Did Marie Curie ask "why?" when she . . .'

'Just go, Alex, or we'll be here until Christmas,' Sammie urged.

So, I got up and sang the first two verses of 'One more Step'. I was a bit quiet to begin with because I was worried everyone would think I was teacher's pet but by the end of the chorus my voice took over, as it always does. The tune was so easy to follow and so jolly to sing I couldn't help but let the words bounce out of me. I even forgot about pizzas for a second.

Everyone joined in the third verse and I admit the singing was loads better after that. Afterwards, everyone clapped, including the parents outside. The bell went and Sammie grinned at me and said 'Nice one, Aretha,' as we both dashed for our bags and coats.

We didn't get very far, though. I'd just gathered up my bag when Mr Sharkey called me over to the piano. I glanced at Sammie, hoping she'd come too, but she just shook her head. Any other topic she'd have waited but not this one. Food was her specialist subject. 'I'll save you a place,' she promised.

'And pineapple chunks,' I called after her. A pizza isn't a pizza without pineapple chunks and I knew Mum, who was one of the After School club helpers, hadn't put many in the airtight containers this morning.

'I will,' she promised, dashing off as Mr Sharkey approached.

'That was wonderful, Alex,' Mr Sharkey praised.

'Thanks, Mr Sharkey,' I murmured, my eyes gazing longingly at the swinging double doors.

He glanced round, stroking his beard thoughtfully. 'Er . . . are you in a hurry to get to the Nut in the Hut tonight?' he asked, meaning Mrs Fryston, my After School club supervisor and *his* bride-to-be. I wondered if he'd still call her that once they were married.

'Kind of,' I admitted.

'Well, I won't keep you but I've got a favour to ask. Would you mind waiting in my office?

Mrs Moore will let you in.'

'Will it take long, Mr Sharkey?' I asked him.

'Two minutes, two minutes,' Mr Sharkey promised, first thanking Mrs Pisarski for her time before striding across the hall to collar one of the teaching assistants.

Two minutes. So likely.

Chapter Two

In the office, I wasn't sure whether I was allowed to take a seat or not; it's not a room in which I've spent a lot of time, thank goodness.

'Just make yourself at home but don't touch anything or read any of the private matters on Mr Sharkey's desk,' Mrs Moore said snappishly, closing the door behind me and going back to her duties on the other side of the glass partition.

'I won't,' I said, crossing my arms in case she dusted for fingerprints afterwards.

I glanced around. On top of a filing cabinet

nearest to me was a Wakefield Wildcats beaker with dried coffee drips down the outside and next to that was a wooden framed photograph of Mrs Fryston, smiling like mad into the camera, with Anna and Kate, her teenage daughters. Anna was the taller of the two and the eldest— I think she's in the same year as Caitlin so she must be eighteen. Kate's in Year Eleven, so she must be about sixteen. They weren't smiling. In fact, they looked really grumpy, as if posing for a picture was the worst thing ever. Mum had told me—well, not me, exactly, but I had been in the room when she was telling Dad—that they weren't very happy about Mrs Fryston marrying Mr Sharkey. Mum never said why, though, and I daren't ask as I shouldn't have been listening in the first place.

'Ah, Alex, sorry to have kept you waiting,' Mr Sharkey said, taking me by surprise. I quickly twisted my head away from the photograph, not wanting him to think I was being a nosy parker. 'Sit,' he instructed, indicating the swivel chair by his desk.

'Thanks,' I said, hesitating to take his seat at first but then enjoying the experience. It was a lovely chair, all soft and squidgy black leather.

'Now,' Mr Sharkey began, picking up his coffee mug and sighing hard when he realized it was empty, before continuing. 'I don't know whether you've heard or not but I'm getting married on the twenty-ninth.'

Was he kidding me? 'Sir,' I said, 'the whole school knows! I mean, you do mention it every morning in assembly.'

'Do I?' he asked innocently, his cheeks turning a pleased pink. 'Well, anyway, as you probably know, we're keeping the ceremony fairly simple . . .'

I nodded. I understood simple. Besides, Mum and Dad had been invited. I probably knew more about the wedding being held in the grounds of Nostell Priory than he did, to be honest. Mum had talked about nothing else for months.

Mr Sharkey's eyes darted towards the glass partition, then back to me. 'But I wanted to do something as a surprise for Jan,' he continued in a much lower voice.

'That's a good idea. Women like things like that,' I said, lowering my voice too.

Mr Sharkey seemed grateful for my support. 'Well, I was wondering whether you'd like to sing for us?'

'Who, me?' I asked, taken aback.

His eyes twinkled. 'Yes, you. Who better? You've got such a lovely voice, Alex, you really have, and we both know you, so it would mean more to us than hiring some stranger. In fact, I'd rather have you than Olenka Drapan herself.'

'Oh,' I said, blushing at the compliment. Olenka Drapan is a Yorkshire legend.

'I was thinking "Pie Jesu" just after we've exchanged marriage vows would be appropriate. What do you think?'

'Fine by me,' I said, warming to the idea. I loved weddings; people wore such elegant clothes and Nostell Priory was supposed to be really posh. I'd fit right in.

Mr Sharkey glanced over my head towards the glass partition again and whispered that it had to be top secret. He looked at me, his mood serious. 'Capital T, capital S, Alex. I want it to be a complete surprise for Jan. I'd prefer it if you didn't even tell your parents. Not just yet, anyway, with your mum and Jan being so close. We'll have to work on an alibi for getting you there on the day, of course. What I thought was if . . .'

Before he could finish, Mrs Moore slid open the glass partition with such a thud it nearly came out of its runner and announced the governors had arrived for the meeting.

'Marvellous,' Mr Sharkey said, rubbing his hands together, 'that means I might get a decent cup of coffee.'

'Wouldn't bank on it,' Mrs Moore replied drily.

I had a final swivel on the

chair, gathered my bits and pieces, and headed for After School club. Alex McCormack, wedding singer. Has a ring to it, doesn't it?

Chapter Three

Excited, and humming the chorus to 'Pie Jesu', which I already knew because I had sung it at chapel for a wedding only a few weeks ago, I hurried across the playground and over to the After School club, which meets in a tatty old mobile hut on the edge of the playground.

Outside the mobile, I automatically stopped humming, paused and had a quick squint through the half-open door. I didn't want to go barging straight in. Everyone knows the hardest part of keeping any secret is right at the beginning when it's brand new and you haven't found a hiding place for it in your brain yet. I was right to be cautious. Guess who was the first person I saw? Only Mrs Fryston, playing Giant Snakes and Ladders almost under my nose! Taking a deep breath, I told myself to think only of pizzas, pineapple chunks, and more pizzas, pushed open the door and entered.

Quickly, I dumped my coat in the cloakroom and went to do what I had to do first—report to Mrs Fryston. As I said, she was crouched down near the Giant Snakes 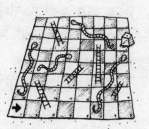 and Ladders mat, her sleek grey hair swaying neatly as she threw the mammoth green latex dice across the floor. 'A two! Oh no! Right back to the start,' she groaned. The younger ones laughed gleefully.

'You're really rubbish at this, Mrs Fryston,' six-year-old Brandon Petty told her happily. He hadn't cottoned on that she often lost on purpose.

'You're right, Brandon, I am,' Mrs Fryston agreed, laughing with him.

I tapped Mrs Fryston lightly on the shoulder, aiming for a quick getaway. 'Hi, Miss, I'm here,' I announced, preparing to zoom off, but she caught hold of my arm and used me to lever herself up.

'Alex! In the nick of time!' she said, walking me over to her desk to cross me off the register. She put a tiny tick in the column next to my name and smiled. 'All aboard for Wednesday. How are you?'

'I'm good, thanks.'

She smiled. She was wearing her coral pink lipstick today and deep green eye shadow. Mrs Fryston always knew how to complement her hair and skin tones; unlike my mum, who never wore make-up full stop, but that's another story. 'How was choir?' Mrs Fryston asked.

'Er . . . you know . . . same as ever.' Please don't make me have a conversation, I thought. I was still finding a hiding place for the secret.

'Mr Sharkey didn't make you work too hard?' she asked, twiddling with her engagement ring, which was white gold with a small, solitaire diamond in the centre for those of you interested in jewellery.

'No,' I said, glancing wildly round so she wouldn't see my face change colour.

Still she didn't let me go. 'Sammie told me he'd kept you back. He wasn't bullying you into singing solo in assembly or anything was he?'

Oh-oh. Too close for comfort. 'Nah,' I said, as cool as you can do when your face is on fire, 'it was nothing really.'

Luckily Mrs Fryston accepted my answer with another smile. I think she just liked hearing about her fiancé. It is amazing how sloppy people in love get. Caitlin's just the same with her boyfriend, Simon. It's not good enough to say, 'Simon called when you were out.' She has to know what he said and how he said it and what colour socks he was wearing while he said it. It does my head in.

'Oh well,' Mrs Fryston sighed dreamily, 'I think Sammie's saved you a seat over at the pizza parlour.'

'Great,' I said, striding rapidly away.

Chapter Four

I said hello to Mum but didn't hug her or anything—I like being treated like everyone else when I come here. Besides, she had flour all down her apron and greasy hands from where she'd been oiling the baking trays. That was on top of her cardigan being buttoned up wrong and her trousers being too short. I expect you are gathering that my mum wasn't exactly what you'd call fashionable, which wouldn't matter to me so much if I wasn't planning a future in the fashion design industry. 'I had a funny feeling you'd be joining my group today,' she grinned at me. 'Find a place, love. You know what to do.'

I did indeed. I'd been coming here for four years, so I ought to.

There weren't many kids at the table—only Sammie, Lloyd Fountain, and Ruby Glazzard. Mind you, having Ruby in the group was like having ten normal children. She's like a firecracker that goes off in all directions, sparks flying, over the slightest thing. Mrs Fryston banned her once because she threw a boot at the back of Tasmim Aulach's head but she's been allowed back to the club, providing she stays on her best behaviour. Best behaviour at four years old! Still, the little demon seemed quiet enough now so I risked sitting next to her and opposite Lloyd and Sammie.

Sammie was going at her dough mix with gusto, her hands sending out vast puffs of flour as she kneaded. 'Hiya,' she said, glancing up momentarily, her tongue pressed to the side of her mouth in concentration, 'I saved you those,' she said, nodding towards a saucer full of pineapple cubes in front of her.

'Oh, thanks, Sammie,' I said, reaching across and sliding the dish towards me, relieved she was so engrossed in her task she didn't ask why Mr Sharkey had kept me behind.

'We can only have six pineapple chunks each,' Ruby told me sternly.

'Yeah, just like you've got,' Lloyd pointed out. I glanced at Ruby's pizza to see what he meant. Pineapple cubes were tumbling from her base—mountains of them—along with fistfuls of onion and cheese. I didn't say anything; life's too short. Luckily, Ruby has the attention span of a buttercup so she soon cantered off to try something else when Mum said the oven wasn't warm enough to cook the pizzas yet, which was good as it meant I could hitch up closer to Lloyd.

Lloyd is my favourite After School clubber. We know each other from Sunday School, so we go way back, but the best thing about him is that he isn't afraid to talk about things that are interesting, like ghosts and death.

'So have you managed to get in touch with your grandad yet?' I asked him, returning to our conversation from the day before. He'd been telling me how he missed talking to his grandad, who had died suddenly last Christmas, and I told him he could just talk to him anyway, like I do to Daniel. Daniel is my brother—you know—the one I mentioned earlier whose New Year resolution was to get a tattoo? He died before I was born, worst luck. He'd be fifteen now if it wasn't for that stupid meningitis. Anyhow, I talk to him all the time at home.

Lloyd began to spread tomato paste on top of his pizza base, plastering the surface with smooth, carefully planted strokes. He draws in pen just as neatly and just as precisely. 'Not really. I tried but it felt weird,' he said.

I nodded. 'Yeah, it does at first but you get used to it,' I told him. 'Keep at it.'

I'd only been doing it myself for a few months. It took a while to get beyond boring stuff like the weather but now I can talk to Dan about anything. We have really interesting conversations.

Our latest one was on whether they had holidays in Heaven. I was just about to tell Lloyd that when Mum leaned over to inform us the oven was ready for the first pizza and I clammed up. Mum can be quite emotional about Daniel so I have to be careful. I didn't want to upset her while she was working.

'Well, my pizza is going to kick ass!' I said instead, which got me a warning about 'language' from her and a grin from Lloyd and Sammie.

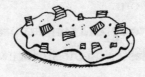

Chapter Five

Caitlin came for me just as my pizza was going into the oven; she always collects me on her way home from college. I tried not to grimace at her baggy purple cords and grungy lime-green top, which did nothing for her apple-shaped frame—she takes after Mum on the bad taste in clothes front—and just grinned instead. I love having my big sister collect me; it makes me feel special. Besides, it means I don't have to stay on after everyone has gone and wait for ages while Mum tidies up and plans things with Mrs Fryston.

'Hi, Caitlin,' I said, 'I'm just waiting for my

McCormack Masterpiece to cook.'

Caitlin looked at her watch and gave me an apologetic wrinkle of her nose. 'Well, you'll have to walk back with Mum then. Sorry, pal, but I've got stacks of work to do.'

Oh no! The last thing I wanted was to be around at the end of the session. Mr Sharkey always came across for a chat. Knowing him, he was bound to wink at me or something and I'd go beetroot and give the game away on day one. 'Ten minutes, please, Caitlin,' I pleaded, 'some of the pizza's for you anyway; I've put extra pepperoni on.'

Caitlin looked at me sorrowfully. 'Tempting, Alex, but no deal. I've got too much to do before Simon comes to take me for a driving lesson.' Blooming Simon.

'Please, Caitlin,' I begged again. The annoying part was that my house was only a bit away—I could have walked home alone if they'd let me but it was against the safety regulations.

My sister shook her head. I knew she wasn't being mean on purpose; I'd seen the textbooks

on her desk. They were thick, glossy, and nasty looking. I didn't even understand some of the titles, let alone what was inside.

'Is there a problem?' Mrs Fryston asked. She had been standing by the ovens, supervising them, while Mum helped anyone interested make a second pizza to finish off the ingredients.

'No,' I said miserably, resigning myself to overtime.

Mrs Fryston scratched at a shard of burnt cheese on the oven mitt she was holding. 'I can walk you across, Alex, if that would help. We're not busy tonight.' Brandon, Tasmim, and Lloyd had already been picked up so she was right about that but even so it was an unusual offer. I looked at her doubtfully.

'That'd be great, Mrs Fryston. Thanks,' Caitlin said for me, then hesitated when she saw the look on my face. 'Is that OK with you, Al?'

'I guess so,' I said slowly.

'See you later then.'

Well, don't break your neck in your rush to get out, sister, I thought, as she disappeared faster than an Olympic sprinter.

As soon as my pizza had cooled enough to be carried, Mrs Fryston escorted me home. It was a warm evening and pink cherry blossom blown from the school field covered the playground like confetti. I wish I hadn't thought of confetti; it made me nervous.

'That pizza smells delicious, Alex,' Mrs Fryston said as we walked round the outside of the school and towards the gates.

'I know.'

'Are you going to eat it straight away while it's still warm?'

'You bet! Pizza's my favourite.'

'I'm more of a pasta girl myself when it comes to Italian.'

'Oh,' I said.

We'd reached the library now. Only a few more

metres then we'd be on Zetland Avenue itself and the pedestrian crossing and, once we were over that, my house. Told you it wasn't far. Now was it my imagination or had Mrs Fryston slowed down? 'Alex,' she said, glancing behind her. She *had* slowed down. We were at a snail's pace—and a tired snail at that.

'Alex, I must confess to an ulterior motive for walking you home,' Mrs Fryston began.

Uh-oh.

'I just want to run this idea I've had by you.'

Let it be about After School club, I thought to myself, but I had a funny feeling in my stomach.

'Well, you know I'm getting married on the twenty-ninth?'

'Yes.'

The funny feeling turned into an unfunny, churning sensation.

'Well, I've been trying to think of how I can make the ceremony a little more special. Not that it isn't going to be special anyway, of course; we're writing the ceremony ourselves, but I want some-

31

thing a bit different. I had asked Anna and Kate to do a reading but they . . . they weren't so keen.'

'Aha,' I said, thinking I bet they weren't. I could just see their glum faces refusing point blank.

'Well, you know how Andrew—Mr Sharkey—is so musical—and he is so proud of you I wondered whether . . .'

We had stopped walking altogether now. Mrs Fryston beamed at me. My arms prickled and it had nothing to do with the heat from the pizza. '. . . you would like to sing at the wedding?' she finished.

'Sing at the wedding?' I said in a croaky voice.

'Yes. It would just be perfect.' She laid her hand momentarily on my arm. 'I thought "Morning Has Broken" right after the vows would be just the right place. We'd need to keep it quiet, though, so it will be a surprise for Andrew.'

Right there, right then, was when I had my own bottle bank moment.

Chapter Six

'Well,' I said to Daniel as soon as I got in, 'what a mess!'

'What is?'

I fetched a clean tissue and began to polish the top of the turquoise lacquered box in which Daniel's ashes were kept. He has pride of place on the mantelpiece, lording it between school photographs, a pair of wooden elephants, and the wedding invitation.

'First Mr Sharkey asks me to sing at his wedding but to keep it secret . . .'

'Oh yeah?'

'Then Mrs Fryston asks me to sing at her wedding but to keep it secret.'

'Oh, very popular. Hang on—isn't that the same wedding? I've been propping the invitation up for weeks! It's blocking my view of the telly.'

'Exactly,' I said, 'the same wedding to sing at the same time but—and here's the good bit—' I said, moving the invitation over to the right of his ashes, 'not the same song.'

'Ah.'

'Now what am I going to do?'

'Don't ask me.'

'You could help,' I admonished, giving him another wipe with the tissue.

'Alex! Will you stop doing that! It freaks me out!' Caitlin snapped from behind me.

I twisted round from the mantelpiece to find her staring at me in disgust. 'Doing what?' I asked, though I knew perfectly well.

'Doing that talking-to-Daniel thing.'

'How much did you hear?' I asked, thinking I'd blown the secrets already.

She scowled at me. 'Hear? Nothing! You don't

actually think I *want* to listen in, do you? I just know you're doing it; that's bad enough.'

'What's wrong with talking to Daniel?' I asked.

Caitlin rolled her eyes at me. 'You know what.'

'I don't.'

'It's not right.'

'Why not?'

'It just isn't, so stop it!' she said and tramped off down the hallway.

I followed her into the kitchen. 'I only talk to him in the living room and the kitchen. I don't do it outside or anything.'

She removed a granary loaf from the bread bin and began slicing it hurriedly in thick, uneven pieces. 'It's still weird,' she said, opening the fridge door and bringing out cheese and a jar of tomato chutney. 'An imaginary friend's one thing, a dead boy you've never even met is another.'

'Well, you lot were the ones who made me

35

say goodnight to him all my life,' I said in my defence, 'all I'm doing is extending the conversation.'

Caitlin waved a knife-full of chutney at me. 'Alex! Pack it in!' she snapped, her eyes narrowed in warning. Oh, it was annoying the way she took out her essay-stress on me.

'Is that all you're having to eat?' I said, promptly changing the subject. I have found changing the subject is the only thing to do in these circumstances. 'I thought you were having pizza with me.'

'I'm not in a pizza mood,' she replied curtly.

'Well, I am,' I said and reached for a slice.

Caitlin didn't even stay in the kitchen to eat with me. She took her sandwich upstairs, along with a bag of crisps and an apple, muttering that she hated Keats. Keats isn't someone she knows. He's a dead poet who wrote rubbish; that's what she says anyway.

I sighed and slid my pizza on to a plate. More for me, I thought, but do you know, after all the fuss I'd made about it, the McCormack

Masterpiece was disgusting. Not hot enough, not enough cheese, and the juice from the pineapple chunks had made the base soggy. I ate half then shoved the remainder to the side and made myself a cheese sandwich too. I had some serious thinking to do and I couldn't do it on an empty stomach.

Chapter Seven

I spent a restless night trying to think of a solution to my wedding song dilemma. Should I choose 'Pie Jesu' or 'Morning Has Broken?' I mean, Mr Sharkey had asked first, so it should be 'Pie Jesu', but Mrs Fryston's the bride and the wedding day is all about the bride, isn't it? Or what if I did one verse of one then one verse of another? No, that wouldn't work—too confusing. Maybe I should just not turn up at all! I knew that wasn't an option, though. I couldn't let them down like that, especially with Anna and Kate already being mean. I liked Mr Sharkey and Mrs

Fryston loads; I would just have to think of a way of pleasing them both. Trouble was, I couldn't, and in the end I gave up and began doodling down ideas for Daniel's tattoo instead.

Next day, Mr Sharkey called me out of maths to tell me Mrs Pisarski was going to stay behind every Wednesday after choir to help me learn the tune and words to his song. I didn't tell him I already knew it. I just said, 'Fine,' and gave him a tight, probably not very convincing, smile but he didn't notice. He'd already moved on to tell Mr Idle, my teacher, about something else.

At After School club, Mrs Fryston pounced on me as soon as I entered the mobile and handed me a photocopy of the words to *her* song. I said, 'Fine,' and gave her a tight, probably not very convincing, smile, too. She didn't dwell on my fake smile either; she didn't have time. Ruby had decided to paint the yellow bean bags with blue poster paint and needed to be stopped. It was the first time I'd been glad Ruby was an After School clubber. As I watched her being hauled over to the sink to wash her paint-covered hands, it occurred to me I had almost another four weeks of keeping up pretences in front of Mrs Fryston. School was bad enough but at least Mr Sharkey and I weren't in the same room much. Here she was . . . well . . . here.

The thing to do was find distractions, I told myself, especially distractions that didn't involve weddings. Ghosts and death, that's what I needed. I glanced around for Lloyd.

He was over in Boff Corner with Brody, Reggie, Sam, and Sammie. They were all huddled over the table, their heads locked in a scrum, when I approached. 'Hi,' I said and they stopped whispering instantly. I was immediately worried then because I thought they must have been talking about me—it wouldn't have been the first time—but they just looked relieved when they turned and saw it was me. 'Oh, hi, Alex,' Brody said in her usual friendly way, 'what gives?'

'Er . . . I wanted just to talk to Lloyd, if that's OK. In private?'

'Oooh,' Reggie, Brody's boyfriend, teased, nudging Lloyd's elbow, 'in *private*. You're in there, my son.'

Do you know, for a Year Seven, Reggie Glazzard's really immature. I don't know what Brody sees in him.

In the book corner, which is enclosed on three sides and the only place in the mobile you are safe from prying eyes and pricking ears, I asked Lloyd a favour. From my school bag, I pulled out sketches I had drawn last night for Daniel's tattoo. Daniel had taken months to decide on the design and finally decided on a crescent moon surrounded by five stars but I couldn't get them to look right. 'My moon looks more like a bent sausage,' I said after I'd explained what I'd been trying to do. 'I wondered if you'd help me, seeing as you're such an ace artist. Please?'

'Er . . . OK,' he said, taking my sheet and frowning.

'Is it that bad?' I asked.

Lloyd frowned again then looked up at me. 'No, it's not that. I'll do it—no problem. I was just wondering if I could ask you something, too . . .' He swallowed hard, making the shark's tooth necklace he was wearing bobble up and down at his throat. Lloyd had a lot of interesting accessories.

'Ask away!' I prompted.

He looked embarrassed and rubbed the side of his neck. 'No, it's about photographs; oh, it doesn't matter.'

'Tell me.'

'Well, I was just wondering whether . . .' His voice trailed away and instead of finishing his sentence, he said he'd better be getting back to the others. 'Why don't you come, too?' he asked.

I shook my head; huddling up with Reggie and

co. was not my thing. 'No thanks. Caitlin will be here any minute and she'll be mad if I'm not ready,' I said.

Lloyd began whispering to me. 'Maybe tomorrow then? We're talking about what to do on the twenty-eighth; we could do with more ideas.'

'The twenty-eighth?' I asked.

Lloyd glanced around, checking no one was listening. 'You know, the last day before Mrs Fryston gets married. We want to do something big for her and Mr Sharkey. So far we've got Reggie and Brody acting out a short play they've written and I'm doing some magic tricks and Sam's reading out a poem and Sammie's put you and her down to sing a duet,' Lloyd continued.

'She's what?' I said, louder than I had intended.

'We're only at the planning stage; there's nothing definite yet,' Lloyd said hastily. 'Sammie'll talk to you about it later.'

I groaned.

'What's wrong?' Lloyd asked.

'Nothing,' I mumbled, 'nothing.'

He knew I was fibbing. 'It's just you're so good at singing . . .'

'I know I am,' I sighed, wishing I was good at something else instead; something *unusable* at weddings. Quickly, I checked my watch—four-thirty, thank goodness. Caitlin would be here any second. 'I'd better get my stuff together. See you!'

'See you,' Lloyd said, a puzzled look on his face.

I could feel him staring after me as I careered out of the book corner and  dashed across to the cloakroom but I didn't care. More singing? Unbelievable!

Chapter Eight

Sammie cornered me the next day in the dining hall, dropping her tray down beside me with a clatter, even though I told her I was saving the last place at the table for Jennifer Wilkinson. Jennifer's in my class and would have been my best schoolfriend, if I'd been doing best school-friends this year. Sammie didn't budge; just grinned at Jennifer when she arrived, who then had to go across and sit with the Year Twos.

'Got to talk to you 'bout something,' Sammie said, immediately stuffing her mouth full of spaghetti bolognese.

'Yeah, I know.'

She eyed me through her frizzy fringe. 'Lloyd told you already, didn't he?'

I nodded, trying not to look at her bulging cheeks.

'He said you didn't seem right keen on the singing idea.'

'It's not that, it's just . . .'

'Thing is,' Sammie interrupted between sucking in an enormous mouthful of spaghetti that put me right off mine, 'Brody wants us all to do something that matches our skills but I can't write and I can't act and I can't draw and Reggie's decided seeing as the whole idea was his—as if—he's going to do the narration all the way through so that only leaves me with singing and even then I'm not that brilliant, as you know . . .'

She finally paused, waiting for me to either agree or disagree with her. I just sat there, trying to think of an excuse for not doing the duet but my brain was too full already and nothing would come.

Not that Sammie was listening anyway. 'You're the one that I want,' she whispered.

'I know but . . .'

'No, that's the song we're going to sing. "You're the One that I Want"—you know—from the musical *Grease*. I'll be Sandy, the girl, you can be Danny, the boy. I've got it on my karaoke CD if you don't know it.'

I sighed heavily, relieved that at least it was just a pop song she'd chosen and not 'Pie Jesu' or 'Morning Has Broken'. 'All right,' I said, 'I'll sing with you.' I mean, it would only lead to a million awkward questions and dirty looks from everyone at After School club if I didn't, wouldn't it?

Sammie beamed, wiped her mouth free of meat sauce with the back of her hand and burped before leaning towards me. 'Don't forget it's a secret,' she said.

Chapter Nine

Now I had three secrets on the go! Thank goodness it was Friday, that's all I could say. I decided on the way home that, even if I couldn't keep my mid-week life simple, I could at least keep weekends simple. I gave myself permission not to think about school, After School club, choir, weddings, or secrets for two whole days. That plan worked—not!

On Saturday morning Mum didn't come down to breakfast. Usually she makes the Saturday breakfast and Dad does Sunday. Instead I brewed the tea while Caitlin boiled three eggs and butchered the bread again. It was all a bit of a rush because Dad had to get to work at the estate agent's he manages and Caitlin had to get to her Saturday job at the Cyber Café and nothing was ready. 'She's having a lie-in; she didn't sleep well last night,' Dad said when I asked why Mum wasn't up.

'Daniel?' Caitlin asked.

'More than likely,' Dad replied softly. 'Grandma phoned up to warn us she'd put a notice for Daniel in the "In Memoriam" column of the paper for the wrong date and it'll be in next week instead of next month, so that set Mum back.' That meant May the fourteenth instead of June the fourteenth, the day Daniel died.

I shook my head. 'Daniel hates it that Mum still gets so upset. He wishes she'd move on,' I said, carefully pouring the tea.

'Shut up, Know-nothing!' Caitlin flared, throwing my egg into my egg cup so it almost fell out again.

'Well, he does!' I said. 'It breaks his heart.'

'Dad! Tell her!' Caitlin demanded.

Dad sighed, chopping the top off his egg with an expert shot. 'Caitlin, what have I told *you*?' he said wearily.

Her eyes blazed. 'Ignore it, you said, it's a phase, you said. Well, it's a blooming long phase!'

'You wet your bed for five years,' Dad retorted, winking at me.

'That is not the same thing and you know it!' Caitlin argued back, her cheeks flushing with indignation. Honestly, what a fuss. Dad looked at Caitlin, looked at me, then looked at the clock. 'Alex, if Mum isn't up by nine-thirty, take her a cup of tea and tell her you're going shopping.'

'What, food shopping?' I said miserably. I hate food shopping. There's nothing more boring in the world than queuing up to put carrots in a plastic bag. When I'm older, I'll do all my food shopping over the Internet and have it delivered straight to my fridge.

Luckily, Dad meant the good kind of shopping. 'Remind her she needs something for the wedding,' he said. 'Tell her we can't do it next weekend as planned because I'm . . . I'm having to value a vast property near Ackworth and it'll take all day. Viv dropped it on me last night and I forgot to mention it.' He bit into his toast, looking pleased. 'And . . .' he added, warming to the topic now, 'tell her to splash out, no expense spared. Dress, shoes, handbag, the lot. Then make sure she has lunch in town; spin the day out as long as you can so she's away from the house.'

'That's a good idea,' Caitlin said, more evenly. 'Keep her occupied.'

Now those were the sort of orders I could live with.

Mum was really reluctant at first, saying things like she didn't feel like going into town and how, anyway, she'd planned on wearing that dress she bought last summer that she's only worn once. I just stood over her at her bedside and kept on at her, though, telling her she'd look a proper fright amongst Mrs Fryston's smart friends and how it was her duty to look beautiful for such a special occasion. Eventually she gave in and she got up, got dressed, and we caught the bus into town.

Of course, we had an argument within minutes of arriving because I wanted her to get something up-to-date and she wanted something boring in lilac that old ladies wear. 'You know I'm not comfortable in things like that,' she said as we walked past all the trendy window displays in the Ridings Centre. Honestly! You wouldn't think it to look at her now but she used to wear brilliant clothes once; she just lost all interest in her appearance after Daniel died. Daniel didn't tell me that, I just know from before-and-after photographs.

Anyway, in this poky little dress shop off the

Bull Ring, my mum tried on one lilac, pink, or pale blue monster after another. 'Oh, I wish I'd never brought you!' she said in exasperation when she showed me the latest disaster and I made out I was going to throw up.

'Well, it's not my fault if you keep choosing horrible outfits that don't suit you one bit!' I explained. Mum flounced back into the changing room while the shop assistant, a tall woman with a mole above her eyebrow, gave me a seriously sour look.

'I know just how Jan feels now,' Mum said, her voice muffled behind the heavy beige curtain.

'What do you mean?'

'Anna and Kate have been less than helpful over her outfit, too. In fact, they refused to even go with her to help her choose hers.'

'Why? Mrs Fryston has good fashion sense. She'd go in the decent shops,' I said. 'No offence.'

Mum wasn't offended—that's the problem. 'Do you know, they've told Jan they're turning up in jeans and trainers, if they turn up at all. Poor Jan; she was so upset. She wants the day to go so well but they seem determined to ruin it for her.'

'Some jeans can look quite smart if they're worn with a sharp top,' I pointed out.

'Not to a wedding, surely?'

'Mmm, well, I suppose.'

'And you'd better not think of wearing black on the day, either.'

'What?' I said, my heart racing. 'What do you mean?'

'When you sing.'

I nearly died on the spot. Here I am trying to keep everything secret and she comes right out with it, in public, where anyone could have been listening. Luckily, I didn't think Mr Sharkey hung out in ladies' changing rooms. 'So you know about that? Who told you?'

'Jan, of course,' Mum said, emerging from the changing room with her blouse half in, half out of her skirt and her hair all mussed up. She flicked at her skirt impatiently. 'Don't worry, I know she wants to keep it hush-hush from Andrew. I think it's a lovely idea.' She gave me a lopsided smile.

'I'll be so proud. "Morning Has Broken", too. One of my favourites.'

'It might not be that one,' I said hesitantly.

'Oh, it is,' Mum told me matter-of-factly, pushing the curtain back, ready for the next customer, 'Jan distinctly told me. Do you mean you haven't been practising?'

'No, it's not that,' I mumbled.

Mum eyed me suspiciously. 'You haven't, have you? I haven't heard you once, come to think of it . . .'

That's because I've been practising in secret because I thought it was a secret, mother!

'I'd better make sure you're up to scratch. I'll go through it with you when we get home,' Mum continued, whisking me out of the shop past the disapproving assistant, 'can't have you out of tune for your special moment. Remind me to get your dad to dig out the camcorder, too . . .'

'Not the camcorder,' I groaned, thinking the whole episode was going to be traumatic enough without capturing it on blinking film.

'Don't be silly,' Mum said, turning left and walking ahead with a spring in her step all of a sudden. I began to wish I'd left her in bed.

Knowing Mum knew about the wedding song should have made it easier for me; at least one secret could be shared. I didn't feel any happier, though, just more mixed up. Now it felt as if I didn't have a choice at all; I had to sing 'Morning Has Broken' at the wedding. How was I going to be able to look Mr Sharkey and Mrs Pisarski in the face next Wednesday when I sang 'Pie Jesu' knowing that? I sighed and hurried after my mum.

After a few more attempts, Mum found this plain linen dress in yukky lilac from a shop further along but she did get some quite smart, pointy shoes to match. The real shock was she let me choose a colourful scarf and long dangly earrings for her afterwards from Accessorize, to go with everything, which for my mum was a bit of a breakthrough. She even bought me a really mint hair clip to wear on the day; it had a diamanté stud at the end of it, 'To make you shine even more,' Mum said proudly.

Dad was dead proud of me, too, when he got in from work. Mum couldn't wait to give everyone a twirl in her new outfit and she seemed upbeat and happy, which was totally opposite to when he had left this morning.

'Good job done, pal,' he said, winking at me and pressing a two pound coin into my hand.

'Thanks,' I said, my throat all dry from singing 'Morning Has Broken' a thousand times that afternoon.

Chapter Ten

OK then, so I had just Sunday for not thinking about school, After School club, choir, weddings, and secrets. That should have been a doddle. I had Sunday School first thing. No chance of anything happening there to trip me up, was there? Ha!

It began well enough. Lloyd's mum, Tanis, is our Sunday School teacher. I like her; she's always friendly and chirpy and allows us to call her Tanis, not Mrs Fountain, so when she asked me to stay behind to help clear away at the end I didn't mind at all. 'Actually, Alex, I wanted a word,' she said when the last of the children, including Lloyd, had headed towards the Wesley Room for refreshments. I thought he might have stayed; I hadn't had a chance to chat to him all morning. He'd been sitting at the opposite end of the room from me, helping Jamie Smith, who has Down's Syndrome, with his sticker book.

'What was the word then, Tanis?' I said, trying to find space in the fusty-smelling cupboard for the last pot of coloured pencils.

Tanis hesitated. 'Actually, no, I think I'll wait until your mum comes,' she said.

There was something in her tone that worried me. 'My mum?' I said, turning round.

She rubbed at a mark on her purple T-shirt. 'Yes, I think that I should,' she said and smiled in a reassuring way that worried me even more because I didn't know why she had to be reassuring.

When Mum arrived to collect me, Tanis began by pulling a sheet of paper from her bag and showing it to her. 'What is it?' Mum asked, puzzled.

'I found Lloyd drawing it last night. It's a tattoo design, apparently . . .'

'Yes?'

'For Daniel.'

'It's brilliant!' I said, taking hold of one corner of the sheet and admiring the perfectly drawn crescent and stars which were  so much better than I could have ever done.

'For Daniel?' Mum said slowly.

'Yes,' I went blundering on, 'now don't get mad but he wants a tattoo. You know what teenagers are like.'

Mum looked at me blankly, not knowing what to say. 'It's not just that,' Tanis continued, turning to me this time. She gave me that reassuring smile again and bent slightly towards me. 'Alex,' she asked gently, 'did you ask Lloyd to find a picture of his grandad to show to Daniel in Heaven?'

'No,' I said, wondering if that's what he'd been trying to tell me on Friday, 'but it's a genius idea!

Daniel doesn't know everybody up there, you see. The photograph will be kind of like getting some ID.'

I heard Mum gasp but Tanis's expression didn't alter; she just kept right on looking at me through her steady blue eyes. 'The thing is, Alex, Lloyd tried to take the photograph his grandma keeps by her bed of Grandad. She was very upset, especially when Lloyd told her what it was for.'

'Oh no,' Mum began.

'He didn't have to take that one,' I said defensively. 'Any would have done.'

Tanis then turned to Mum. 'Sorry, Ann; I know this is tricky for you, but can you deal with this? You know how we're struggling at home with Mum since Da died, and with Lloyd, for that matter. This kind of thing doesn't help.'

'No,' said Mum, her face pale now, 'no, of course it doesn't. I'm sorry, Tanis.'

'Alex,' Tanis said, giving me the picture of the tattoo, 'please don't ask Lloyd to do things like this any more, OK? I have explained to him that when someone dies their spirit goes up to Heaven but there is no direct contact on earth from the dead. They cannot talk to you. That's what we believe in our family, OK, and I'd like it if you respected that?'

'OK,' I mumbled.

'Thank you,' she said.

Although Tanis had been calm and pleasant about the photograph and everything, I still felt as if I had done something seriously wrong, especially when Mum didn't say a word all the way back. When I asked her something she'd turn to look at me but not say anything. She'd just stare at me through eyes that looked hollow and empty, like the pushed-in windows of a used Advent calendar.

Chapter Eleven

As soon as we got home, Mum went straight upstairs to her bedroom. 'What's the matter?' Dad asked, drying his hands on the tea towel and glancing worriedly over my shoulder.

I explained what had happened and he closed his eyes, then rubbed them tiredly. 'I'll go take her a cup of tea,' he said, leaving me alone with Caitlin.

She'd been flicking through the Sunday papers, not seeming that interested in what I'd been saying, but as soon as Dad had left the kitchen she started. 'Tattoos? Photos? Are you nuts?' she hissed.

'No.'

'This time of year, too! Poor Mum! I don't believe you sometimes.'

'No one's asking you to,' I said defiantly, reaching towards the comic section of the paper. Caitlin slammed her hand down hard on top of mine.

'Ouch!' I yelled, shaking my hand which stung like mad.

Instead of apologizing like she should have, Caitlin gave me a really nasty look and pulled the comic section out of reach. 'You'd better stop all this now, Alex. It's not funny any more.'

'Who's laughing?' I said.

'Not me for a start,' she grunted and headed off to her bedroom too.

I didn't see Caitlin for the rest of the day. I heard her telling Dad she couldn't stand being round the house and she called Simon and he picked her up. She wouldn't even stay for dinner, which is a shame because she missed Dad's brilliant roast chicken with cranberry sauce. I ate every bit. What's more, so did Mum, who came downstairs after her rest and looked loads better. Instead of pretending nothing had happened like she sometimes does, Mum actually talked to me about the photograph incident too. 'It would have broken my heart if someone had taken Daniel's photograph from me at the time,' she said. 'Lloyd's grandma hasn't got much else to cling to.'

I said I was sorry and that I'd talk to Lloyd about it at After School club. She seemed satisfied with that.

I thought everything would be OK then but when Caitlin wasn't back by my bedtime and when Dad came into the bathroom while I was brushing my teeth and started messing about with the towels on the towel rails behind me, even though they were perfectly straight already, I knew I was in for another Tanis-type moment. 'Alex,' he said quietly.

I couldn't answer because I had a mouthful of froth so I just went 'hmmph'.

'I think it might be a good idea if you don't ... er ... talk to Daniel any more ... or at least not for a while.'

I spat into the sink. 'Why not?' I asked.

'I think you know why.'

Turning round, I couldn't help scowling at him. 'I said sorry to Mum at dinnertime and she said it was all right, didn't she? And Caitlin's just stressed because of her stupid exams,' I said.

'I know but ...' Dad paused, passed me a towel to wipe my mouth on, then continued solemnly. 'But there's no point upsetting them while they're feeling a bit fragile, eh, pal?' he said.

'Can't I talk to Daniel ever again then?' I pursued, feeling a bit weepy at the prospect.

Dad gave me a short, sad smile. 'Best not for a while at least, Alex. Best not.'

'Fine,' I said gruffly and handed him back the towel.

'And,' Dad said, 'Caitlin won't be picking you up from After School club during her exam time. She wants to stay on and work in the library.'

I looked at him and he looked at me. We both knew what a fib that was.

I was in such a mood when I talked to Daniel for the last time that night. '. . . and she's now decided she's not even picking me up from the club! Working in the school library. I do know! She's always complaining about how kids mess around in there and she can't concentrate! It's all a pack of lies. She's really got it in for me and I don't know why. As if I haven't got enough to worry about . . .'

Daniel calmed me down and he said he bet that when the exams and the anniversary of his death were over and done with, we could start again from where we left off and nobody would bat an eyelid. He also told me not to worry about him because he had plenty to do; Elvis was giving a concert and Daniel had been asked to help supervise the knicker-throwing from the ladies in the audience. 'And I'll be there to watch over you at the wedding; I promise,' he said.

I felt a little better when he told me that, but not much.

Chapter Twelve

Caitlin hardly talked to me at breakfast, pretending to be reading poetry, even when I told her I'd stopped talking to Daniel. 'So?' she said, not bothering to look up at me. 'You should never have started in the first place.'

That did it! I was trying my best and she just wasn't giving an inch. I mean, I hadn't even told Dad about her hitting me. It was all one way with her. 'Oh, be like that, then!' I said, throwing down my cereal spoon and leaving her to her stupid Keats.

I felt horrible all day, though. I hate falling out

with people, especially my only sister who I usually got on fine with; it makes me feel funny, as if something has been taken out of my insides and put back the wrong way up. I managed to get through school all right—there was so much to do—but when Mum came to collect me for After School club I felt all miserable again and I broke my own rule by holding her hand all the way across the playground. She didn't say anything, just squeezed it back, so I knew she didn't bear me any grudges for yesterday.

I couldn't bank on Lloyd not bearing grudges, though. What if he wasn't talking to me either, like Caitlin, for getting him into trouble over the dead people thing? I'd hate to lose him as an ally at After School club. Thing is, despite going there the longest, I wasn't exactly one of the in-crowd at After School club. Apart from when Jolene comes during the summer holidays, Lloyd is the only one on my wavelength.

As soon as I entered the mobile, I searched for him. It didn't take long to find him as he was wearing his long, brightly coloured rainbow jumper which made him stand out a mile. Luckily, he was alone at the computers, so I went up to him and sat on the chair next to his, pulling it close so we weren't overheard. He turned and smiled shyly at me, which was a relief. I opened my mouth, about to apologize, but instead of letting me say sorry to him, he said sorry to me first. 'I daren't even look at you in Sunday School because I knew what was coming. I feel really bad I didn't hang about to stick up for you.'

'It doesn't matter,' I said, 'I'd have done the same, probably.'

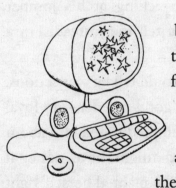

He lowered his eyes and began picking at a loose thread on his jumper. 'I felt like a jerk for dropping you in it.'

'Why? You didn't do anything wrong. I think the photo idea was a mint one. Daniel said so, too.'

Lloyd looked up at me, a furious glint in his eye. 'That's what I tried telling them but they wouldn't listen! Gran's been in hysterics, ranting about me being disrespectful to Grandad's memory and how he'd be so disappointed in me.'

I opened my mouth in protest. 'Oh, you are not disrespectful! Everyone knows how much you loved your grandad! It's not fair the way everybody else is allowed to tell us what dead people do but we're not allowed our own ideas,' I said hotly, thinking of Caitlin. 'I've been banned from talking to Daniel now, you know, and there's so much I need to ask him about some problems I've got.'

'Well,' Lloyd began, picking at his jumper again, 'maybe you could tell me instead. I'm a good listener.'

I looked at him and I could tell he was serious. He was right, he was a good listener, and loyal too. I was really, really tempted to tell him about the wedding thing, and might have done, if Sammie hadn't arrived. She planted herself right behind us and just stood there grinning, this soppy look spread all over her chops. 'If you can tear yourself away from your girlfriend, Lloyd, we've got a meeting,' she said. At the mention of the word 'girlfriend' Lloyd and I sprang apart like a baby bird's beak at feeding time.

Lloyd began closing down the computer and I frowned at Sammie who just smirked. 'You can join us if you like, Alex,' she offered.

I had planned to e-mail Jolene and was going to say 'no' automatically but then I heard Brody laughing at something and I thought I wouldn't actually mind being with people who were cheerful for once. 'OK,' I said, 'count me in.'

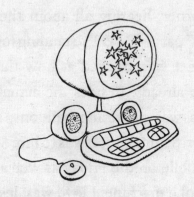

Chapter Thirteen

Two minutes later, I was huddled over the table in Boff Corner, hearing all about the plans for the 'WOTY' party—WOTY standing for Wedding of the Year. I was amazed at how much they'd thought up already. Besides the actual perform-ances, Sam was providing balloons, streamers, and banners, Sammie's job was to lure Mr Sharkey into the mobile on the Friday as well as bringing in her karaoke machine, Lloyd was designing the box in which to put all the gifts, Brody was bringing food, and Reggie had arranged for a special congratulations announcement to be read out on the local radio station, Radio Fantastico. They were really going to town. 'OK,' Reggie continued, 'all we need to do is fix the rehearsal times . . .'

'Rehearsals?' I asked.

'Yeah, we can't exactly practise the acts here, can we? Some surprise that would be! Can everyone make it to Brody's on Saturdays?'

'Mine?' Brody asked.

Reggie removed his glasses, cleaned the lenses using Brody's tie, then continued. 'Well, come to mine then, if you want Ruby Dooby-doo interrupting every three seconds . . .'

'Point taken,' Brody nodded. 'We can—'

'WOTY alert!' Reggie suddenly announced and everyone sat bolt upright. Lloyd began drawing, Sam and Sammie started poring over a comic, and Reggie started spouting French at Brody. I quickly folded my arms and looked innocent as Mrs Fryston came up to us and asked if we were all OK.

'We're champion, love,' Reggie told her with a cheeky grin.

'Yep, definitely all right, love,' we all chorused, nodding like maniacs.

Mrs Fryston shook her head as if she didn't know what to do with us. 'There are spaces on the craft table with Mrs McCormack if anyone wants to make chocolate cookies,' she said.

'Nah,' Reggie replied, 'too much homework. But if anyone wants me to test theirs out for 'em after, I will do.'

'Oh, Reggie,' Mrs Fryston smiled, 'ever the joker.'

Now that we knew we'd be rehearsing at Brody's there was no need to huddle over the table any more. Sam went to set up the refreshments stall with Sammie, Reggie and Brody really did start their homework, and Lloyd began reading *The Horse and his Boy*. I went on the computer and e-mailed Jolene, telling her all about the plans for the WOTY party, knowing nobody would read what I'd sent.

Even staying on later didn't bother me that much. Sammie stayed on, too, because her dad was one of the helpers, so while the grown-ups gathered in one corner and talked about the schedule for the following day, Sammie and I scooted off to the cloakrooms and talked about our schedule for the following Saturday. It was the best fun I'd had at After School club for ages. I told Caitlin so as soon as I got home and she just looked at me and said, 'Good'.

Chapter Fourteen

I will say one thing for having a complicated life instead of a simple one; time goes fast. All too soon, a week had gone by and Wednesday had come round again. That meant my 'Pie Jesu' practice with Mrs Pisarski. I had stomach cramps all day, worrying about that moment when choir practice finished and Mr Sharkey said to me, 'Alex, have you got a minute?' What if Sammie decided she'd stay behind this time and I had to explain to her what was going on? What if Mrs Fryston walked past and accidentally heard me? What if I got my lines mixed up and sang bits of 'Morning Has Broken' instead?

As it turned out, none of those things happened, apart from Mr Sharkey asking me to stay behind. Sammie just shrugged and disappeared again—I'd forgotten Tasmim's mum was coming in to make onion bhajis so naturally she just shrugged and disappeared again! Mr Sharkey made sure Mrs Fryston didn't accidentally hear me by going over to the mobile himself and staying there with her for forty minutes, and I didn't mess up on 'Pie Jesu'.

In fact, I did the opposite; I sang it really well. 'Pie Jesu' is one of those songs you can't help but give your all to; the lyrics and tune fill you with this power that can't be ignored. I'm glad I was already familiar with it, though, as some of the notes were difficult to hold. Even so, at the end, Mrs Pisarski looked at me, her eyes moist, and told me I'd done wonderfully. 'Alex, there will not be a dry eye in the house when you have finished,' she declared softly. 'I only wish I could be there but I have to work in the shop.' Mrs Pisarski and her husband run the corner shop on Zetland Avenue and Saturdays are their busiest days. 'You are giving the perfect blessing with your beautiful voice,' she continued, 'Andrew will be so, so proud of you.' I bowed my head then, wishing it could be so. Deep down, I preferred 'Pie Jesu' to 'Morning Has Broken' and would have loved to have sung it at the wedding.

I went to After School club lost in thought, imagining the perfect scenario for the twenty-ninth. Perhaps if I just launched straight into 'Pie Jesu' immediately after I'd finished Mrs Fryston's hymn? They'd both be happy then, wouldn't they? After the initial surprise wore off? I mean, they were bound to realize what had happened straight away and then they'd both just laugh about it, wouldn't they? 'You are not going to believe this!' Mrs Fryston—no, Mrs Sharkey—would explain to all the guests. Wouldn't she?

I had a weird dream that night that wasn't quite as comforting. The vows had just been exchanged and I stepped forward from behind some curtains—they were the curtains from that horrible dress shop—and everybody looked at me. To my left, unexpectedly, was Mrs Pisarski on the piano, hands raised, ready to begin, and to my right was Mum with the photocopied sheet of 'Morning Has Broken', shaking it at me like an over-enthusiastic charity collector with her tin. I opened my mouth to sing but nothing would come. People stared at each other and started whispering. Then they began to give me a slow hand-clap, each clap sounding like a smack against someone's cheek. Louder and louder it got; then the jeers started. I kept turning from Mrs Pisarski to Mum until I became so dizzy I fell to the floor. I woke up then, luckily still in my bed but feeling nervous and shaky all the same. If it hadn't been so dark on the landing, I'd have gone downstairs and talked to Daniel, whatever Caitlin said. If it hadn't been so dark.

Chapter Fifteen

I didn't have any bad dreams after the Saturday rehearsal at Brody's house, thank goodness. That was much more fun. For a start, it was at Brody's place, which is amazing. It's this huge old sandstone house built high up from the road so it seems like miles from the gate to the front door. The room we were rehearsing in had wooden panelling on the walls and these seats which fitted into the recess beneath the window that could sit three people easily. Even the downstairs loo was bigger than our bathroom at home and it had all these framed photographs on the wall Brody's dad had taken of famous models and actors—he's an important photographer, in case you didn't know. I'd have spent all my time in there if I could have got away with it.

As well as having an amazing house, Brody's mum had laid out wicked food for us. There were jugs of fresh fruit juices we could pour for ourselves into cocktail glasses, complete with crushed ice *and* umbrellas *and* bendy straws. There were sandwiches and home-made popcorn and, in the centre, this monstrous glass bowl full of white and pink marshmallows. Sammie's eyes nearly popped out of her head when she saw them. Party time!

We had to earn our treats, though. The Wedding of the Year performance had to be spot-on as far as Brody and Reggie were concerned. Especially Reggie. Now Reggie gets on my nerves sometimes because he always has to be the centre of attention but he had really taken his role as co-ordinator seriously. He didn't mock when Lloyd messed up his trick with the disappearing feather duster, just told him not to worry and to try again. He didn't make snoring noises when Sam's poem dragged on to its fifth page— just told him it was brilliant but went over the time limit so to chop it down a bit. He *did* laugh when Sammie and I performed our song but then he was meant to—we were playing it for laughs. Reggie even produced a false beard for me to wear so the audience would know exactly who I was meant to be when I sang 'You're the One that I Want' with Sammie.

I almost skipped down the long driveway at the end of the first rehearsal. The WOTY party was going to be brilliant and I was glad I was part of it.

Chapter Sixteen

The following week was more or less the same, except for at home because Caitlin had begun her exams. I thought she might have gone into a massive stress and was ready to keep well out of her way but instead she seemed quite calm and more relaxed than I'd seen her in ages. Even after a three-hour exam she seemed—well—normal. Even after the one on Keats! 'What will be will be,' she just shrugged. Go figure, as Brody would say.

Mum seemed fine, too, even though the anniversary of Daniel's death was drawing closer.

Usually she would be taking her special tablets now, to get her through, but I'd checked and the foil wrappers had remained intact. 'It must be this wedding lark distracting her,' Dad had suggested when I'd pointed it out. I wished I could be as laid-back.

Mr Sharkey came into assembly on the Monday before the wedding, rubbed his hands together and asked, 'Well, children, only five more days to go to what earth-shattering event?'

'Half-term?' one of the teachers teased.

'Apart from that,' Mr Sharkey replied.

'Your wedding!' Brandon shouted out from the front.

'Got it in one, young man! Would my knees be shaking like this just for half-term? I don't think so. But I will be on my honeymoon by then so maybe they should be! Yikes!' Mr Sharkey then made everyone laugh by knocking his knees together comically. Trouble was, my knees really were shaking—I didn't have to act.

After assembly, Mr Sharkey waited for my class to file past and collared me as I tried to leave the hall. 'See you in choir on Wednesday, Alex,' he said, very chirpily for such a nervous man.

'Yes, sir,' I replied quietly.

He glanced over my shoulder to check no one was listening. 'We'll need to finalize travel arrangements and everything,' he said.

'Sure,' I mumbled, glancing quickly down at my sandals. I couldn't tell him arrangements had already been made—Anna and Kate had been ordered to pick me up at the house at twelve o'clock. Mrs Fryston thought it was best for me not to arrive with Mum and Dad, to keep it all separate. She also reckoned giving her daughters something specific to do would stop her from strangling them. The nearer it got to the wedding, the more sullen and uncooperative they were becoming, she'd told Mum, especially Anna. It was going to be one interesting car journey to Nostell Priory, that was for sure.

This time, I had the bad dream before Wednesday's choir practice instead of after it. In the dream, I'd just finished singing 'Morning Has Broken' but before I could launch into 'Pie Jesu',

Mr Sharkey went nuts. His face turned a deep, ugly purple and he began tearing at his beard in outrage. 'How dare you! How dare you ruin my big day?' he shrieked.

'She made me do it! She made me do it!' I cried, pointing with a shaky hand towards his wife.

'Leave the Nut in the Hut out of this!' he bellowed back.

I woke up in bed in a horrible sweat, breathing hard, my heartbeat thumping in my ear. I think I must have cried out, too, because Mum rushed in to ask what was wrong and stayed until I went back to sleep again, stroking my hair across my forehead like she used to when I was little. I can't swear to it, but I'm sure she called me Daniel instead of Alex just before I drifted off.

Chapter Seventeen

That last Wednesday was a long, long day but then somehow not long enough. All too soon it was time for choir practice. Sammie immediately shouldered her way to stand next to me, grinning and tapping her pocket every two minutes as if putting out a small fire. I knew she was excited because it was her job to get the WOTY party plan started by giving Mr Sharkey a bogus invitation to After School club this Friday.

All through choir practice, my lunch churned slowly and uncomfortably in my stomach like a sluggish cement mixer that had been filled with gravel by mistake. I couldn't focus at all on the songs we were practising; I kept thinking of afterwards. Never mind being a wonderful singer; I was going to have to be a wonderful actor to get through this, I thought.

Sammie didn't help by prolonging the agony. At the end, when everyone had been dismissed, she marched straight up to Mr Sharkey and handed over the invitation. 'This is for you, Mr Sharkey. Open it!' she said, a huge beam on her face.

'OK,' he said, playing along and reading the invitation out loud. 'Hmm, "*UR invited 2 ZAPS After School Club on Friday aft @ 4.15 prompt 2 judge the decorated biscuit competition 4 the Food Glorious Food theme*". Mmm. An invitation part English, part maths. How unusual.'

'Prompt,' Sammie reminded him, 'there's a lot to get through.' She nudged me in the ribs as if to say, 'And don't we know it!'

Mr Sharkey nodded and

broke into a smile. 'I'd be delighted to judge the biscuits. Do I need to bring any special implements with me? Hammer and chisel perhaps?'

'No!' Sammie sniffed. 'Though you might want to avoid the green ones Brandon made. They've got spinach in.'

'Spinach? Knowing Brandon's fondness for all things green, it could have been a lot worse,' Mr Sharkey said signalling to Mrs Pisarski we were ready to start. 'Right then, Sammie, off you go— I just want a word with Alex.'

Sammie shrugged. ''S all right, I'll wait. We're not making nothing tonight.'

'Well, you don't want to be late for Mrs F— you know how she worries.'

Sammie just waved her hand dismissively. 'Oh, she won't miss me for two minutes—not with Ruby to chase after.'

Mr Sharkey began to get a bit impatient. 'Well, when I said two minutes, I meant a bit longer than that. I need Alex to . . . tidy up the music trolley.'

'I'll help,' Sammie offered.

'It doesn't take two people to sort out a few maracas and tambourines,' Mr Sharkey said lightly but firmly, steering Sammie over to the doors. Sammie frowned at me over her shoulder and I just shrugged as if to say, 'Sorry'.

This time when I sang 'Pie Jesu' I was rubbish. Really, really rubbish. I struggled to hold the difficult notes and Mrs Pisarski had to keep stopping and say, 'Concentrate, dear, concentrate.'

It would have made my life a whole lot easier if Mr Sharkey had said, 'Oh, heck, Alex, you're not up to scratch, girl. Perhaps we'd better cancel Saturday,' but he didn't. Instead, he just put my performance down to nerves and said I'd be 'all right on the night' which Mrs Pisarski backed up by saying I'd been wonderful the week before and would be on the day 'without a doubt'.

After Mrs Pisarski had left, we went into his office. Luckily Mrs Moore wasn't around so there was no need to whisper today. 'Now, about getting to Nostell,' he began, 'we're obviously going to have to let your parents know what's happening . . .'

'Oh no,' I interrupted, ready with my lie, 'we don't! Mum'll only fuss like mad if she knows so I want to just appear. Caitlin's going to bring me—she's passed her driving test now and needs the practice in her new car. She'll sneak me in without everyone seeing. It's all sorted.'

'Oh!' he said, a surprised look on his face. 'Well, I suppose that's one less problem to worry about!'

After that he went into great detail about where exactly the ceremony was being held, how to get there without being noticed, listening out for cues in the service.

'Now, the ceremony itself is being held in a huge marquee in the grounds—you can't miss it! If you enter from the back where . . .'

I listened and nodded, hoping I looked as if I was taking it all in and hadn't heard it all before from Mrs Fryston at the end of After School club two days ago.

When I finally got to After School club, I approached Sammie cautiously, wondering if she had the hump with me for staying behind. She was helping Sam serve on the sweet stall, so I queued up behind Tasmim, Ruby, and Lloyd, thinking I'd better check her out, to be on the safe side. While I waited, I said hello to Lloyd. He said hello but that was about it. Since the Sunday School incident, our conversations had become a bit stilted unless we were discussing the WOTY, which we couldn't do here. 'See you,' he said to me when he'd been served.

'See you,' I replied, then asked for a ten p mix.

'What mix do you want? Cola bottles or lemon chews? Raspberry bombs or fizzy bears?' Sam asked.

'Anything as long as it's not shaped like a musical instrument,' I groaned.

'Was it boring?' Sammie asked.

I nodded hard, pretending I was really cheesed off about tidying the music trolley. 'Not half! I don't know why Mr Sharkey wouldn't let you help—I could have been much quicker,' I said.

'That's just what I said to Sam,' Sammie agreed, 'Mr Sharkey's never liked me.'

'Oh, I don't think it's personal,' I said hurriedly.

Sammie just shrugged. 'Whatever,' she said and threw an extra lemon chew into my bag. 'What?' she said to Sam when he reminded her about his profit margin.

Chapter Eighteen

Then it was Friday. I didn't mind Friday at all. After School club could come round as quickly as it wanted, even though I knew it was going to be pandemonium. 'Got your beard?' Sammie whispered to me on the way over.

'Yeah!' I said, patting my carrier bag. 'Got your karaoke machine?'

Sammie nodded. 'Better have, anyway. Dad should have sneaked it in to the mobile earlier.'

'It's going to be great,' I said, excitedly squeezing Sammie's arm.

'What is?' Mum said, overhearing. I hadn't

mentioned the WOTY party to her at all, though some of the other mums knew because they were helping out.

'Oh, nothing, Mrs McCormack,' Sammie replied, then snorted into her hand. Sam Riley, who had been right behind us, gave Sammie a warning prod.

'Just the biscuit testing thing Mr Sharkey's coming over to do,' I told Mum, thinking I'd better say something to explain why we were being what she called 'giddy'.

Mum paused, one hand on the Reception class's door handle she'd been about to twist, and frowned. 'Yes,' she said, a puzzled tone in her voice, 'I don't know why Brody and Reggie wanted to make such a thing of those biscuits. We're making chocolate boxes next week; I would have thought they'd have been more interesting to judge, if anything. Two of the parents have even turned up to watch—Tanis and your mum, Sam.'

We all glanced at each other. That meant Lloyd's

box with the gifts was here, and Sam's mum's donation of party poppers and balloons from her card shop. So far so good.

Mum continued, still trying to fathom it. 'I don't know what they're expecting to see—nor does Mrs Fryston. Half the biscuits have already broken anyway and the rest are made of spinach.'

'Oh, you know what mums are like,' Sam said calmly, 'mention food or wine and they're over like a shot.'

'Well, there's certainly no wine,' poor Mum began, 'but . . .'

'Is my dad there, too?' Sammie interrupted.

Mum nodded. 'He was. He just dropped something off for you then left again.'

'Yee-ha!' Sammie laughed, punching the air.

Mum shot Sammie a despairing look. 'Oh dear, Sammie,' Mum said, finally entering Ruby's classroom, 'you won't be too loud this afternoon will you? I've had a long day.'

'Me, Mrs McCormack?' Sammie laughed. 'I'll be as good as gold.'

Chapter Nineteen

At first, everything was pretty normal-looking in the mobile, apart from the extra mums. My mum delivered the nine or so of us attending from Zetland Avenue and handed over her register to Mrs Fryston while we all dumped our stuff in the cloakrooms and went to find a warm-up activity to do like a puzzle or something. Apart from Sammie being a bit hyper, no one else was saying or doing anything out of the ordinary. It helped that the committee had not told any of the younger ones about today; not to be mean, just because we knew kids like Brandon couldn't keep secrets. This first half hour before Mr Sharkey arrived was crucial to the whole thing— it had to go as smoothly as possible—especially as Brody and Reggie arrived after us and were relying on Lloyd, Sam, Sammie, and me to get the ball rolling.

Pretending to carry on as normal, I helped wheel the sweet stall into the refreshment corner with Sam while Sammie fetched the tubs of sweets and biscuits from the store cupboard. Lloyd, over by the computers with Tasmim and Brandon, glanced across at us and nodded briefly. 'Five minutes,' Sam said, looking at his watch as I opened a tub of Lemonade Bombs.

'Don't count down,' I said. 'I'm feeling really nervous as it is.'

'Four,' Sam said, ignoring me totally.

'The bus lot are here,' Sammie announced, dropping more tubs on the stall with a thud and darting off again. The bus lot were kids from other schools who were bussed in to ZAPS After School club. Once they had dumped their stuff, Mrs Fryston would sit everyone down and go through any news and tell us what our options were for the activities that afternoon. Or so she thought.

'Two,' Sam said, as Mrs Fryston clapped her hands together and asked us all to gather on the carpet.

'Don't count down!' I repeated, edging my way to the front so I could sit next to Lloyd, who had saved spaces for all of us.

'One,' Sam hissed, plonking down on the other side of me.

'Well, good afternoon, everybody,' Mrs Fryston beamed. She was looking really pretty today in her short-sleeved blue blouse and cream coloured trousers and dangly amber earrings. I thought how nice she'd look on the DVD Brody's mum was going to make of the whole thing. Mrs Fryston paused, bent down to confiscate one of the Ker-Plunk sticks Ruby was plunging into her toy giraffe's eye, then smiled again. 'OK, as you know, a little later we're going to have the decorated biscuit competition so if there are any late entries, get them finished quickly. Before that, though . . .' Mrs Fryston stopped, her attention drawn to someone. I held my breath but didn't turn round. 'Can I help you, Mrs Moore?' Mrs Fryston asked.

At the mention of Mrs Moore's name, I pinched Lloyd's arm and Sam pinched mine.

'And we're off!' Sam whispered.

'There's a telephone call for you over in main school, Mrs Fryston,' Mrs Moore said curtly. She hated taking messages for After School club.

'Main school? Couldn't you give the caller my mobile number?' Mrs Fryston asked.

'Oh, I tried, believe me. I also reminded the caller that school and After School club were two separate bodies and I was not at the beck and call of either.' See what I mean?

'Well, I do mention that fact on my newsletter home every time,' Mrs Fryston pointed out, 'but it would be lovely if you could just take the number and ask if I could call back in five minutes.'

'Oh, I tried that. Apparently it's most urgent and most personal.'

Sam elbowed me again.

'Oh,' Mrs Fryston said, looking worried now and turning to Mum. 'Er . . . Mrs McCormack, could you finish off for me here while I just pop across and take this call?'

'Oh, yes of course,' Mum said, looking flustered. Being suddenly put in charge had caught her out but I knew she didn't have to worry. Her role wouldn't last long.

'And GO!' Sam announced, jumping up when he had made sure Mrs Fryston was safely out of sight.

Once we'd got rid of Mrs Fryston with the bogus phone call from Sammie's dad about his voluntary hours at the club, the next twenty minutes were like something out of a clip from *You've Been Framed* put on fast-forward. I took Mum to one side and explained what we were doing while Sam told the kids. They all cheered and started mucking in with us, helping to clear spaces so we could perform. Tanis and Sam's mum, Sarah, immediately began dishing out streamers and party hats, Sammie set up her karaoke machine, and Lloyd began getting his podium thing assembled for his tricks. A few minutes later, Brody and Reggie arrived with Brody's mum, each carrying a large cardboard box full of food.

'Goodness me!' Mum said, looking a bit bemused by all the frenzy.

'Well, you didn't think we'd not do nothing for them, did you?' Sammie asked, pulling up her pair of borrowed leather trousers for when we sang our song, then stepping hurriedly out of her school skirt and stuffing it in her empty karaoke machine box.

'Well, I did wonder about organizing something,' Mum said lamely, 'but I wasn't sure how to go about it.'

Sammie clapped her hand on my mum's back. 'Don't worry about it, Mrs M. Just leave it to the experts.'

Chapter Twenty

Oh, I wish you could have been there! You'd have loved seeing the looks on Mr Sharkey's and Mrs Fryston's faces when they arrived in the mobile together, perfectly timed by Sammie's dad on the phone and by Brody's mum who went over to 'collect' them. Everyone shouted 'Surprise!' followed by an explosion of party poppers and crazy foam and confetti raining down on them. Then Brody led them to the side where her mum had made two thrones from a pair of high-backed wooden chairs and covered them in silver foil and velvet for them to sit upon, like a king and queen.

Mr Wesley had been hiding them in the shed outside all week.

I know I haven't gone into much detail about the contents of the WOTY party so far because I wanted to save it for you until now. It was brilliant! I forgot about everything during that hour and a bit: I had a *ball*.

Reggie, as Mr Sharkey, and Brody, as Mrs Fryston, narrated the whole thing, telling the 'true' story of how they met, and the different 'events' that happened along the way. To make up for not including the other clubbers earlier, Reggie kept inviting them to 'help' him with the story. He addressed his audience, getting the way Mr Sharkey always stands with his shoulders back and feet pointing in opposite directions perfectly. Then, stroking a false beard even longer than mine that he had somehow rigged up to twinkle with miniature fairy lights, he began. 'Now, after our first date, I wanted to give Jan something special as a thank you for taking me to the chippie and buying me those mushy peas,' he told them, 'something nobody else would give. Can you lot think of anything?'

'A diamond necklace!' Tasmim called out.

'What? On my salary? Give me a break!' Reggie retorted, which had the real Mr Sharkey laughing and nodding in agreement.

'A green Chubba Chub lolly?' Brandon suggested.

Reggie nodded. 'Now that's more like it, young man, but I wanted it to be something she can keep. Samuel Shakespeare Riley, can you think of anything?' he said.

'Who me?' Sam asked innocently.

'Yes, you.'

'Well,' Sam said, rising to his feet, 'poetry never fails to woo the ladies.'

'Poetry! Of course. Can you think of anything suitable?'

'Funny you should mention that,' Sam said, pulling out a huge scroll from behind the bean-

bags. It was made from a roll of wallpaper coiled round a gigantic tube of wrapping paper and was so long, he needed two kids from the audience to help him unravel it. 'Ode to the Nut in the Hut . . .' Sam began. Oh, it was so funny, Sam's poem, but moving too. I'm sure I saw Mrs Fryston wipe a tear from the corner of her eye when he'd finished.

Then it was Lloyd's turn to perform some magic tricks (in our version of their courtship, Mr Sharkey took Mrs Fryston to see a magician on the night Mrs Fryston proposes). Lloyd, who'd been taught all he knew by his grandad, performed all his tricks expertly, only fluffing on the disappearing feather duster again but nobody seemed to notice. The action moved quickly on as Brody, wearing a tight skirt and high heels, crouched down on one knee and, holding out a pink plastic ring with a huge 'diamond' on top borrowed from the dressing-up box, asked Mr Sharkey to marry her.

'Me?' Reggie asked, pretending to faint. 'Me? With my dreadful taste in clothes?'

'Yes, you, you hairy lump,' Brody replied, fluttering her eyelids.

'But why?'

'Because you're the one that I want!'

That was mine and Sammie's cue to do our song. We jumped up, got into our starting positions while Lloyd prepared the karaoke machine, and then the two of us danced and sang our way through the *Grease* song. Halfway through my beard fell off and Sammie, getting a bit over-enthusiastic, did one twirl too many and almost ended up squashing Lloyd's podium thing flat. That made Brandon, right at the front, collapse in a heap at my feet because he was laughing so hard, and Mum had to take him out and give him some water to calm him down. Oh, the whole thing was great.

At the end, Mr Sharkey and Mrs Fryston thanked us. 'How did you find out about the

mushy peas on our first date?'
Mr Sharkey wanted to know.

Mrs Fryston, a little more
emotional and blinking back
tears, said what a fantastic
surprise it was and how clever
we'd all been keeping it a secret
from her. 'All this, right under my nose!' she said,
glancing in admiration at Reggie.

Mr Sharkey winked at me then, as if to say,
'There's more where that came from.'

Chapter Twenty-One

Even though it had been a brilliant day, I had the worst nightmare ever that night. This time it was Mrs Fryston shrieking at me for getting the songs muddled and then, for some reason, Daniel's ghost started floating in the air above everybody's heads, making terrifying laughing sounds. It was horrible, horrible. I must have fallen back to sleep though because next time I peered at the alarm clock on my bedside cabinet it was nine o'clock. Nine o'clock on Saturday, the twenty-ninth of May. This was it!

The wedding was at half past one and Anna

and Kate were picking me up at twelve. Sometimes three hours can seem like three weeks but not today; it passed frighteningly quickly. All too soon it was time to get changed into my outfit—plain cotton cropped trousers and a white top with a purple star across the middle. It was nothing too extreme but it felt a bit funny to be out of black. I did like my hairslide a *lot*; that made the outfit, I have to say.

I returned to the kitchen just in time to hear Radio Fantastico play 'You're the One that I Want'. 'This goes out to Mrs Jan Fryston and Mr Andrew Sharkey, from all the kids at Zetland Avenue Primary School After School club with loads of love . . . and that was sent in by Reggie "coolest dude on the planet" Glazzard, it says here,' the DJ laughed.

Mum laughed too, and told Dad that the message was 'typical Reggie'. Then she saw me and clapped her hands together. 'Oh, you look lovely, Alex!' she said, her eyes glistening.

'So do you, Mum,' I replied. I meant it, too. Her new outfit made her look so much younger and sparkly. I almost said, 'Have you shown Daniel?' but stopped myself in time. It was a shame, though, because I know he'd have approved and called her something funny like 'hot momma'. Dad made up for it by taking a zillion photos of her on his digital camera.

Then it was twelve o'clock and the doorbell rang. 'That'll be your lift,' Dad said, running a finger round the inside of his stiff new shirt collar and smiling at me. 'Operation "Morning Has Broken" begins!'

Chapter Twenty-Two

Dad led Anna and Kate into the living room where Mum and I had hastened—Mum exclaiming that the kitchen was too much of a mess for 'guests'. Mrs Fryston's daughters were dressed just how Mum had predicted in the shop that time, in jeans and T-shirts, no make-up, their long, chestnut-brown hair in no particular style. Anna already looked bored but Kate said hello at least.

'Hello,' I replied, thinking how pretty they would have looked if they had made an effort.

'You all look nice,' Kate said, then glanced

round the room, her eyes lingering on the mantel-piece before flicking back to me. Neither Kate or Anna had been to our house before, though Mrs Fryston had been loads of times, for meetings and everything, so they'd know about the ashes. People were always either fascinated or put off by them. I'd guess by her face Kate was of the fascinated variety.

'Right then,' Dad said, looking at his watch. 'All set. Do you know the way, Anna? Or do you want to follow me in my car? That Doncaster Road can be tricky.'

Anna looked offended. 'I think I can manage, thanks.'

Mum didn't say anything about Anna's rude tone but I knew she was annoyed from the look on her face. Dad didn't notice at all. 'OK then, let's go. After you, ladies.'

Anna's car was a shiny black Mini Minor parked down the side of our road. 'Right,' she said after we'd waved Mum and Dad off, 'let's get this farce over and done with.'

'Stop it, Anna,' Kate chastised her.

'Why?' Anna snarled.

'Because we've got company for a start,' Kate said, pulling her seat forward so I could clamber into the back of the car.

'Huh!' Anna replied, in a tone that meant she couldn't care less.

I didn't say anything at first; my mind was set an hour and a half ahead, to that moment straight after the vows, when I would get up to sing. It's no big deal, it's no big deal, they'll laugh about it, they'll laugh about it, I kept saying to myself.

In the front, Anna and Kate continued bickering. 'That way's quicker,' Kate pointed out as Anna missed the junction for the Doncaster Road.

'Who wants to be there quicker?' she bit back, slowing right down as we bounced over speed humps in the street. 'All that faking it.'

'Oh, put another record on, Anna,' Kate protested. 'We've not dressed up, have we? That's protest enough.'

'Is it heck! I wouldn't be going at all if it wasn't for being lumbered . . .'

I knew she meant me and I sat back in my seat as far from the firing range as I could. They carried on like that for ages, making me more and more anxious—I hate arguments. 'You're heading towards Sandal! We don't want Sandal!' Kate yelled.

'Do you wanna drive?' Anna snapped.

'We'll be late!'

'Who cares?'

I cared. The thought of being late terrified me. If I wasn't there in good time, giving me a chance to hide and do my breathing exercises properly, I wouldn't be able to sing a note of either song. Everything would be even worse than it was going to be anyway—everything! I couldn't stand it. 'Stop it!' I cried out, putting my hands over my ears. 'Stop it!'

'Now look what you've done!' Kate said to Anna, twisting round and looking at me anxiously.

Anna slammed on the brakes and abruptly pulled on the handbrake making everyone lurch forward. The car behind beeped loudly as she

halted by the side of the road. 'There! I've stopped it!' she said cockily, reaching for a bottle of water.

'That's not what she meant and you know it,' Kate mumbled.

Anna turned round, too, looking down her nose at me. 'Don't worry, I'll get you there in time for your big number!' she said sarcastically, making an inverted commas sign with her fingers.

That did it! Normally I wouldn't have dared talk to someone so much older than me but Anna Fryston was being horrible and I'd had enough. I sat bolt upright and let her have it, even though I was trembling. 'For your information it's two big numbers actually and at the same time.'

'The same time?' Kate asked, puzzled.

'Yes!' I said, blurting out the whole tale as quickly as I could. 'But the only reason I'm singing at all is because you two wouldn't do the reading Mrs Fryston wanted you to do!' I added, still fuming at Anna's dig at me. 'Mrs Fryston was really hurt, my mum said. She wanted you both to be part of the ceremony and I think Mr Sharkey knew that and that's why he asked me to sing, too, to cover the gap.'

I stopped then, thinking maybe I had gone too far; Mum was always reminding me not to repeat personal things I'd overheard at After School club. 'Er . . . anyway, if you could just get me there on time, please,' I said, leaning back and staring at the terraced houses opposite.

'Chill out, girl,' Anna said, twisting back round and setting off again.

You won't believe this but within seconds the pair of them started arguing *again*, but in much lower voices this time. 'I told you Mum was hurt about that reading,' Kate hissed.

'So?'

'Well, it wouldn't have killed us to do it, would it?'

'Speak for yourself.'

'Alex is right—we have been stroppy. Poor Mum! And poor Andrew. I feel really bad now.'

Anna glanced sideways, giving Kate a

withering look. You could tell she was the same age as Caitlin—she shot perfect deadly daggers. 'Poor Mum nothing! What about poor Dad? How do you think he'd feel?'

'Dad would want her to be happy.'

'Oh, shut up, Kate, you know nothing!' Anna ordered in disgust.

At the mention of 'poor Dad' I pretended I'd gone deaf. Was that what this was all about? They were upset about what their dad would think? Mr Fryston had died of cancer a few years ago when Anna was twelve and Kate ten. He hadn't been that old—about forty, I think, if I remember from my eavesdropping days. Blimey, another dead person complicating things—form a queue, you people!

Nobody spoke again until we finally reached the imposing main entrance to Nostell Priory. It was quarter past one. I had fifteen minutes! My stomach was churning so much, I was scared I was going to throw up. Then the miracle happened.

As Anna indicated to turn left at the gatehouse

and into the grounds, Kate ordered her to head for the overspill car park furthest away from the house instead.

'Why?'

'Because there's been a change of plan.'

'What do you mean?'

'You'll see.' Kate twisted back round to me as an irritated Anna took the new route. 'Alex, this is what we're going to do . . .'

What we did was very simple but got me out of the dilemma that had been haunting me for weeks. I sneaked over to the rear of the huge marquee, as planned, slipping in through the side so no one saw me. Kate went round to the main entrance and told her mum I had arrived, as planned, then when she came back I took up my place behind the billowing curtaining that acted as a backdrop for the ceremony, as planned. It was fortunate both Mr Sharkey and Mrs Fryston had chosen the same hiding place for me or the whole thing would have been blown already. Mr Sharkey, standing at the front with the registrar and looking smart in a light-grey suit, caught sight of me from the corner of his eye and gave me a relieved thumbs up. So far so good.

As soon as the music started my heart leapt. I held my breath all the way through the beginning of the ceremony, listening for my cue, trying not to hop from side to side. I didn't even sneak a peek at Mrs Fryston to see what she was wearing, I was concentrating so hard. Only when the vows had been exchanged, and Kate stepped forward, did I dare move. I inched towards the gap in the backdrop, needing to hear every word and see how everyone reacted.

'Hello, everybody,' Kate said, in a nervous but clear voice, 'this bit's unrehearsed so bear with me, please.'

There were a few murmurs and some rustling of order of service sheets but I kept my attention on Kate. It took a lot of courage to do what she was doing. Anna was sitting much further back, her arms folded defiantly.

By now, I was hardly breathing at all as Kate

turned to Mrs Fryston and Mr Sharkey. 'Hello, Mum; hello, Andrew,' she said to them levelly, 'it's me, the pain in the neck . . .' She paused and tried to smile, clearing her throat quietly for what was to come next. During the pause, Mrs Fryston and Mr Sharkey both looked puzzled and confused. Mrs Fryston even frowned, thinking Kate was going to say something awful, I suppose. Her hand tightened round the binding on the posy of flowers she was carrying; tightened so much the whites of her knuckles showed, even from where I was standing.

She needn't have worried, though. I knew my outburst in the car had made an impression on Kate. I reckon it had given her the courage to do what she did next. Fixing her eyes on Mrs Fryston, she began apologizing in a low, quiet voice that had the guests leaning forward in their seats to catch her words. 'I'm sorry I've been so stubborn over the wedding, Mum. I just kept thinking how cross Dad would be but he wouldn't really, he'd be happy for you and I . . . I am, too . . .' There was a chorus of 'Awww!' from the congregation and Kate's face turned bright red. 'There's something else I have to tell you,' Kate continued, as Mrs Fryston relaxed her grip on the bouquet.

I swallowed hard then, and crossed my hands, pressing them firmly round my sides to stop them shaking. This was it: the moment—my night-mare—live from Nostell Priory. There was a flicker of surprise and disbelief from both of them as Kate told them about the coincidence over the songs. They looked at each other, then glanced towards me, smiling and shaking their heads. It was all exactly as I had imagined—the bad bit followed by the good bit but thanks to Kate acting as a buffer, it meant I didn't feel like *I* was to blame for the bad bit when I was beckoned from my hiding place. I can't begin to describe how relieved that made me feel.

'So here she is. Alex is going to sing two songs for you, both dedicated to Mum and Andrew on their special day.' Kate gave me a wide smile and stood aside. Mr Sharkey, still shaking his head, just grinned as I took my place at the front and Mrs Fryston mouthed 'good luck'.

Feeling like a canary set free from its cage, and pretending I hadn't seen my dad at the back with the camcorder pointed at me, I sang my heart out. I did 'Morning Has Broken' first, followed by 'Pie Jesu', giving it everything I'd got. At the end, everyone clapped really loudly, even Anna, who until then had been sitting with a face like a wet weekend.

When we were talking about the mix-up with the two songs afterwards, Mrs Fryston— wearing this really elegant cream-coloured satinette dress with matching bolero jacket and beautiful drop pearl earrings, by the way—told me it was amazing they hadn't twigged before. 'If Andrew had told the registrar about your song like I did mine, for instance . . .' she said, shaking her head.

'It didn't even occur to me,' he laughed, patting me on the head like I was a puppy.

'Well, I'm just glad it's all over,' I told them with relief.

'Over?' Mr Sharkey protested, his eyes twinkling as he pulled his new wife close. 'It's only just begun.'

Chapter Twenty-Three

Isn't it funny how, when you're dreading something so much, you build it up and build it up for weeks and weeks then the time arrives and it's all over in a flash and you wonder what all the fuss was about! I slept so deeply the night after the wedding, and for so long, I missed Sunday School completely next morning. Instead, I spent most of the day humming to myself and sorting out my room and playing CDs I hadn't played in ages *dead* loud.

I kept re-living the moment I stepped out to sing, adding one or two imaginary moments of my own. 'You thought I was marvellous, Dame Olenka Drapan? Why, thank you! You are most kind!' 'You want me to join your band as a backing singer, Mr Williams? Oh, I couldn't possibly; I have far too much homework to get through . . .' 'A singing contract, Mr Cowell? Let's do lunch. Here's my number . . .'

I was so busy enjoying not feeling anxious now the wedding was over, I forgot Mum would be the opposite. The wedding was over which meant Daniel's anniversary was next. I had been so full of beans, I hadn't noticed Mum wasn't until it was time to go to bed. As I said goodnight to Daniel's ashes, she began sobbing. The sobs came out so unexpectedly and loudly, sounding like an animal in deep pain, I jumped in alarm. 'Such a tiny box,' she said, her shoulders heaving as she tried to stop. I ran over to give her a cuddle; I hate it when she's so upset. I wanted to tell her Daniel got upset, too, seeing her like this and that he was OK, really, but Caitlin was in the room so I daren't. Instead I just held her for a long time until she gave me a watery smile. 'I'm all right, now, love. You get to bed,' she said.

'Will Mum be all right tomorrow?' I asked Dad when he came up to tuck me in.

'At the club? Sure! A bit of sticking and gluing isn't going to trouble my strong lassie.'

'But she's in charge and it's half-term,' I reminded him. Half-term was always harder. The club was open all day and with Mrs Fryston being on her honeymoon, Mum had to be there by half-seven in the morning to set up the breakfast bar. How would she cope with that *and* co-ordinating all the other activities *and* if someone like Ruby got in a foul temper, if she was weepy like this?

'Don't worry,' Dad reassured me, 'your mum's fine as long as she's kept occupied. Remember the day you took her to buy her outfit for the wedding? She was low then but you turned her right round. Just keep half an eye on her; you know my work number, don't you?'

'It's in my address book,' I told him miserably. 'I'll take it with me.'

I spent the whole of Monday watching Mum, checking her out for signs, like if she forgot to do something or if she didn't listen properly or if she seemed edgy. Luckily, she did seem normal, like Dad had said she would be, but I wasn't. In fact, I was the tense, edgy one not concentrating on anything. Part of me didn't mind; if my mum needed me, I was going to be there for her, no sweat, but watching Mum meant I hadn't joined in with one thing anyone had done today. 'I see Alex is keeping life simple again,' I heard Sammie tell Sam when she had asked me to help her first with the breakfast bar, then to set up the new wooden train set, and I'd turned her down both times. 'Leave her; she's a loner,' I had heard Sam reply. No I wasn't! I didn't want them to think that at all. I'd enjoyed being part of the WOTY. I enjoyed being in the gang. I didn't want to be shut out already. That's when I knew I had to do something—quick.

Chapter Twenty-Four

When I got home, I went straight to Caitlin's room. I knocked on her door, just like she insisted, and asked if I could come in. 'OK,' she replied.

She was getting ready to go out with Simon to the cinema. 'What to see?' I asked. I didn't really want to know but I was building up.

'Oh, whatever's on,' she shrugged, trying on a pink velour scarf then throwing it down.

'Put a necklace on instead,' I suggested, 'that one made of all those tortoiseshell buttons; it suits you best and will flatter that neckline.'

'You reckon?' she asked, opening her jewellery box and rummaging round for it.

'Definitely,' I said. If only she watched *How Dare You Wear That?* on telly like I did she'd know about these things.

'This one, yeah?' she stated, dangling the necklace in the air.

'Yep.'

'How was Mum today?' she asked, scowling as she struggled to fasten the tiny catch on her necklace. I sighed heavily as I went to help her. 'Not good?' Caitlin guessed.

I sighed again. 'Not really. Well, she was all right—she didn't cry or anything but—Caitlin, I want to ask you a favour.'

'What?'

I swallowed hard, knowing she wouldn't like what I was about to ask but I reckoned if Kate could stand up to her bossy sister I could stand up to mine.

'I need to talk to Daniel again,' I said, backing away quickly in case.

She sprang round to face me. 'What?'

'Don't get mad. I need to talk to him. I need to ask him something.'

'Like what? Has he met Elvis?' she scoffed.

I was so tempted to tell her he'd met him ages ago but bit my lip. 'No! I want to ask him to tell Mum to stop being upset.'

She was cross with me at first, I could tell. Her mouth tightened and her body stiffened but she didn't shout. Caitlin just looked at me and shook her head. 'You can't do that,' she said eventually.

'Why not?'

'Because the only thing that would stop Mum being upset is if he hadn't died at all.'

I opened my mouth to protest but closed it again because I knew Caitlin was right. Caitlin was always right. 'Have a nice time at the pictures with Simon,' I said miserably and turned to leave.

'Wait a minute, Alex.'

'What?' I asked, wiping my eyes roughly with the back of my hand. I felt all choked up.

Caitlin moved towards me and bent down so we were eye to eye. 'Look,' she said, 'I've been thinking . . . and talking to my psychology teacher and . . . I've been a bit harsh with you over this Daniel thing. He's your brother as much as mine, right? If you want to talk to him, about general things, go ahead. Just as long as you don't—you know—ask impossible things. Especially in front of Mum.'

'Seriously?' I asked, my heart skipping fast. I had missed talking to Daniel more than I realized.

'Seriously,' Caitlin repeated. 'I need to be less possessive over him, less . . . jealous.'

'Jealous?' I asked in astonishment.

'Sure,' she said, straightening up and striding over to her shoulder bag. She began to load it with stuff that was scattered about her dressing table: keys, tissues, purse. 'He never talked to me after he died like he does you. I tried, but he never answered.'

'Oh,' I said, even more astonished, 'I never knew that.'

She cleared her throat. 'Yeah, well, I was only six, remember. Anyway, it's probably important you do start talking to him again,' she continued, 'seeing as you don't seem to be able to talk to me any more.'

Was it my imagination or did she sound a bit hurt when she said that? 'What do you mean?' I asked.

She adjusted her necklace slightly even though it looked fine as it was. 'I could have talked to Anna Fryston about the wedding thing if I'd known about it, you know. We are in the same class for English!'

'You're always too busy or stressed out,' I mumbled defensively. 'You have been since Christmas.'

'That's not true!'

'It is! Why do you think I started talking to Daniel in the first place?'

Caitlin raised her eyebrows. 'You tell me, Alex.'

So I did, because I could remember the moment as clearly as anything. 'It was Boxing Day, right. Mum and Dad were flaked out in front of the telly—which was only showing rubbish—and you had gone to Simon's *again* . . .'

'There's more room at his house,' she protested.

'. . . after you'd promised to play Cranium with me . . .'

'Oh.'

'. . . and I had nothing to do and nobody to talk to. I thought, so this is what it's like being an only child. And if it's like this now, what will it be like when Caitlin goes to university? But then I looked at Daniel on the mantelpiece and it was as if he was saying, "You've always got me, I'm going nowhere," so then I said to him, in my head, "Exciting life, isn't it?" and he went, "Tell me about it—if I hear Charles Dickens bragging about how many times his books have been made into films once more I'll crack up".'

A flicker of a smile crossed Caitlin's face and she nodded. 'So his voice has been more like an imaginary friend thing because you were bored?'

'I suppose,' I said slowly but inside I wasn't so sure. It might have started off that way but it was much stronger than that, but I didn't know how to explain, so I just kept quiet. At least Caitlin was *listening* for once.

She beamed at me. 'I knew it! You need to get out more; come on.' Pulling my hand, she led me downstairs, shouted through to Mum and Dad she was taking me to the pictures and in a flash I was standing in the foyer of the Odeon with her and Simon and holding a gigantic tub of popcorn.

'What do you want to see?' Simon asked, craning his head to squint at the television screens above. Simon, by the way, has terrible dress sense like Caitlin but he's nice so I won't bang on about it.

Caitlin scooped out a handful of my popcorn and squinted at the listings on the screen. 'Find one we can get into with Titch here,' she said, 'as long as it's not that Bruce Willis one where the kid sees dead people!'

'Very funny,' I told her.

'Pity they're not showing *The Wedding Singer*,' Simon added, continuing the joke.

The pair of them then started competing to see what other film titles they could come up with to take the mess out of me and I thought, it's just like being with Reggie and Brody in five years' time. I didn't mind, though. It was still fun playing gooseberry and having my sister back.

Chapter Twenty-Five

After my conversation with Caitlin, and on Dad's advice, I decided not to stress over Mum at After School club. Me fussing round her wouldn't help much anyway, would it? I mean, it was only natural, wasn't it, to be sad around the time your child died? That's the way I'd come to see it, anyway.

The rest of the week, I'd sneak a peek at her from time to time but mostly I just got stuck in to the activities, mixing with everybody. Every morning I kicked off by choosing the outdoor activity. I am not that sporty but Sammie and everyone seemed to want me to join in with them so I thought, why not go with the flow? I was pretty pathetic but by some fluke I got a full rounder once and everyone rushed to give me a high-five; that made me feel great.

In the afternoons, I helped make a monster with Lloyd and Brandon and one of the new kids called Pawel, out of stuff from the re-cycling box. It took three days and by the time we'd finished it was almost touching the ceiling. Unfortunately we didn't stick it together very well so on the last morning of half-term when we arrived we found it splattered all over the floor. 'Yeah!' laughed Brandon. 'Let's make another!'

While we were gathering all the bits of card and egg cartons together, I told Lloyd I was allowed to speak to Daniel again. 'So if there's anything you want me to tell him . . .' I began, then hesitated. 'Sorry,' I said, 'I forgot about your mum . . .'

Lloyd kicked at a ping-pong ball we'd used as an eye and looked at me, his chin tilted. 'Actually, I'm doing my own research into the afterlife at the moment. Mum's not happy but I've asked her what does she expect when she's encouraging me to be an independent thinker?'

'Exactly!'

'Maybe we could get together and have a discussion sometime? I'll show you my findings. I've been very impressed with Miranda D. Feluchi's *Psychic Phenomena Explained*.'

'I'd like that,' I told him, smiling, 'I've missed our talks.'

'Me too,' he said.

That afternoon we finished the half-term holiday perfectly, with Brody bringing in the DVD of the WOTY party her mum had taken.

'That was brilliant!' Reggie said when it was over. 'We rocked that day!'

I looked round at everyone and thought, we did, didn't we? And I rocked the day after, too, but that's another story.

Epilogue

Well, everything settled back down again when Mrs Fryston and Mr Sharkey returned from their honeymoon. At After School club, we finished the 'Food Glorious Food' theme with a Scottish food tasting session. We tried haggis and tablet and crowdie which is a white cheese rolled in oats, but we had to make do without the whisky Reggie requested 'to wash it all down'. We had water from the Highlands Mr Sharkey bought from a garage just outside Wetherby instead.

'Mrs Fryston, are you still Mrs Fryston or are you Mrs Sharkey now?' Brody asked.

'I'm still Mrs Fryston,' she replied, scooping another spoonful of haggis and dropping it on to Sammie's plate. 'I'm too old to change my name. Besides, my girls would never allow it.'

Mrs Fryston glanced at me when she said that, as if sharing something with me. I smiled but I didn't say anything. I guessed I'd be hearing all about how Anna and Kate were taking to Mr Sharkey from Mum later. I had thought about Anna and Kate a lot since the wedding. I knew they still missed their dad and I totally understood why Anna was angry—no one could ever replace my dad if he died, either—but I hoped she wouldn't give Mr Sharkey too much of a hard time. He's such a decent bloke, even when he's in a Sarky Sharkey mood, and life's too short to bear grudges. That's what I had come to realize through all this, anyway. Not simple, but short. Well, unless you believe in reincarnation like Lloyd does now, and then life goes on until you reach something called nirvana, apparently, which can take for ever.

I don't think I believe in reincarnation but I do

know dead people stay around for a long time even if they've had a short life. I don't mean they stay around like ghosts, I mean in people's memories. Take Daniel, right? He died eleven years ago but my mum and dad and sister still miss him like mad and grieve for him, especially around certain times like birthdays and anniversaries. That never goes away.

Mum's mood dipped round the anniversary of Daniel's death, just like we knew it would. She took a couple of days off work and couldn't even force herself to get dressed, she felt so low. It was Caitlin who suggested maybe we ought to think about burying Daniel properly, instead of keeping his ashes on the mantelpiece as a constant reminder.

That surprised all of us because it was Caitlin who, when Daniel had died, hadn't wanted him buried in a grave because she had worried about him being scared of the dark. She had been only six at the time, though, remember.

'What do you think, Alex?' she'd asked me. 'Would Daniel want that now?'

I nodded. 'I think so too,' I said, pleased she had included me.

So that's all being sorted. Mum and Dad have been making arrangements for a plot in the cemetery and we've been designing a headstone for Daniel. I'm hoping maybe a moon and stars will be etched somewhere on the headstone, maybe top right-hand side. It depends if symbols like that are allowed. I haven't asked Dan what he thinks. The weird thing is, since Caitlin said it was OK for me to talk to him again, I somehow haven't got back into the habit. Life's so busy now I'm not keeping it simple any more.

We begin a new theme at After School club  next week called 'Potty Pets' and Mr Sharkey's preparing the choir for a concert at the cathedral in June so we're practising like mad for that. Caitlin's finished her exams now but she's got another driving test coming up soon and I'm helping her learn the Highway Code for her theory part. I don't know the date of the test exactly because she's keeping that to herself but fingers crossed she passes this time. It will be nice for her if she does pass and keeps her New Year resolution.

Talking of resolutions, I'm not saying Dad was wrong when he gave me that advice for mine because it was my own fault I took it to extremes. I mean, only wearing black clothes— what was I thinking? That was definitely a phase I won't be repeating until I'm a fashion designer. Black does *nothing* for girls of my age, unless you balance it with masses of accessories. And keeping friendship groups simple? Not possible. Friendships are always complicated, unless all your friends are hamsters, I suppose. When they are human beings there's always something going on in their lives, like grandads dying or sisters stressing over exams or planning surprise parties for teachers, but that's what makes us interesting. Besides, if things like that didn't happen, I wouldn't have anything to e-mail Jolene about.

Speaking of Jolene, she's coming to After School Club for three weeks during the summer. I can't wait to see her. If there's one thing I can count on, it's that life won't be simple when she's around!

Jolene's Back

—the girl who knows what she wants
(and won't stop till she gets it)

Chapter One

Before I start, if you're a girl reading this, I just want to say something. Last time you heard from me I said I didn't want you to read my stuff if you liked kittens and thought boys were 'cool' and you wore pina colada lip gloss. Well, forget all that. I'm not bothered what you like or what you wear. It's each to their own, isn't it? I'm not going to judge you, just like I wouldn't expect you to judge me because I'm never seen out of my Sunderland AFC shirt and would rather lick a Toon fan's boots than wear lip gloss. No hard feelings then? Mint. Now I've got that off my chest I can start.

Life's a bit mad up here at the moment. Usually when the football season is over I'm a bit lost and bored like, but not this summer term. There's too much going on. I leave primary school this time so there's been loads of stuff to sort out for my new secondary school like uniforms to buy and forms to fill in and bus passes to organize. On top of that there's masses to finish off in class, like taking displays down and project work to chuck away and people to say goodbye to for ever.

Yesterday I had my last session with counsellor-lady. First thing she said to me was, 'Goodness, you've shot up, Jolene!' That's because she hasn't seen me for months now I don't need her anger-management talks as much. 'So, are you looking forward to secondary school?' counsellor-lady asked. 'You're going to The Angel of the North Community College, aren't you? That's a long way to travel.'

Instead of mumbling an answer like I used to

do, I sat up straight and put a bit of feeling into it. 'Way-ay, man, I am going to the Angel! I can't wait, cos they've got a decent girls' football team and an all-weather pitch and a cracking sports hall . . .'

She smiled and nodded as I reeled off the list of sports facilities at the new place, then she said exactly the same thing my teachers have been telling me for months. 'The main thing is it will be a fresh start, Jolene.'

'Yep,' I agreed.

'You can make sure the school notices you for all the right reasons, like Jolene Nevin, captain of the girls' football team instead of Jolene Nevin captain of fighting and flare-ups!'

'I know,' I said, 'except I'll be Jolene Birtley.'

Birtley is Darryl my step-dad's last name. Birtley's not exactly flashy as last names go but it's better than Nevin, any day.

Counsellor-lady scribbled something on her clipboard then looked up and grinned. 'Well, that is progress,' she said. 'A year ago you wouldn't even acknowledge Darryl existed, let alone take his name.'

I couldn't argue with that; she was spot-on. When my mam first got together with Darryl, I couldn't stand him but, well, he kind of grew on me. Now I think Darryl's a top bloke and I love him to bits.

'What about his two boys? Are you still finding them . . .' she glanced at her notes and smiled again, '. . . wet and whingy?'

'Wet and whingy? Did I say that? Nah! They're crackin' lads. Keith's nine now and really into cars big-time and Jack's seven and doing my head in watching *Peter Pan* on DVD every two minutes but no, I get on with them great. Really great.'

'And your mum? How are things with her?' counsellor-lady asks cautiously.

'Yeah, things are great with her and all!' I said, bending down and rummaging in my bag so counsellor-lady wouldn't see my eyes and know I was lying. I quickly found the box of Mr Kipling's almond slices I'd bought for her and stuck it under her nose. 'This is for you, miss, for all your help. It's not much but I'm saving up for a new Sunderland shirt and you know what a rip-off price they are. Sorry they're not wrapped; we ran out of paper.'

'Why, thank you all the same, Jolene,' she said, though she looked a bit puzzled at my choice.

'They're the nearest I could get to currant buns,' I explained. 'Do you remember, you told me to say a rhyme when I thought I was losing it and the sparks started flying and I chose "Five currant 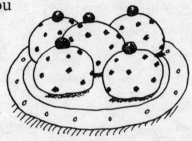 buns in a baker's shop"? Well, we haven't got a baker's shop near us so I had to make do with those from the Co-op instead.'

Counsellor-lady laughed and put the box in her leather bag which was bulging with files. 'I'll treasure them for ever,' she said.

'I wouldn't,' I told her, 'the sell-by date's up the end of this week.'

Anyway, that was yesterday and today's the Leavers' Service and I'm due up on stage any second so I'd best be off.

Chapter Two

The best bit of the Leavers' Service was at the end when we were told we could join our families. I jumped straight off the stage, vaulted over an empty pushchair, and dodged round about twenty-five rows of chairs to get to mine, I did.

They were stood near the back, next to the refreshments. I knew Mam wouldn't be coming—she said it wasn't worth losing a day's holiday for—but there was Darryl, grinning away, with Keith and Jack either side of him, and next to Darryl were my grandad Jake and his wife Kiersten and their twelve-year-old daughter

Brody. Yes, I know that makes Brody my very young auntie. It's Grandad's second marriage, OK? We specialize in them in my family but if I went into all the ins-and-outs we'd be here all day. Anyway, point was, everyone was there I wanted to be there, all right?

'Y'al reet, bonny lass? You were great!' Darryl said as I flew towards him and wrapped my arms round his generous—OK, massive—belly.

'I know!' I laughed, dead pleased to see them all and surprising Grandad and Kiersten by hugging them, too. I wouldn't normally go in for that touchy-feely stuff but this was a special occasion and they had made an effort and come all the way from Wakefield which is a hundred miles from here.

I was hyper all the way home. Not only had I finished primary school for good but Jack, Keith, and me were going to spend five days at Kirkham Lodge, Grandad and Kiersten's place. It would have been longer if Grandad hadn't had to bring his holiday in America forward. Still, five days was better than nothing, especially as we'd be going to Brody's brilliant After School club while we were there. Unfortunately, Grandad Jake was taking Brody and Kiersten to the Lakes for the weekend first. If it had been up to me we'd have set off right now. Still, it gave us time to pack, I suppose. And for Mam to have twenty more rows with Darryl.

It was the rows I was thinking about when counsellor-lady asked how things were with Mam and I'd just said 'great'. Things weren't great at all; they were chronic. Mam started the minute she came home from work just as we were finishing off our dinner. 'Where's Dad?' she snapped.

'They had to book in to the hotel but they did invite us over later for a drink,' Darryl explained opening the cupboard to find a clean plate for her.

'Typical,' Mam said, leaning against the worktop and examining her long nails, 'can't hang on two minutes.'

'It has gone seven, pet. We thought you were coming home at five,' Darryl pointed out.

Mam fixed Darryl with a glare cold enough to freeze the nuts off a squirrel. 'Back at five? I wish! I can't leave the salon, just like that. *I've* got a job with responsibilities.' She tapped the bronze name badge, engraved with her name and rank (assistant manager), which was pinned to her white, body-hugging overall.

CLAIRE BIRTLEY
Assistant Manager

'So what was Queen Kiersten wearing today?' she asked me. 'Some little designer number that cost more than this house, I suppose.'

I shrugged and ran a finger round the rim of my plate to get up the last of the sauce. 'I don't know. I didn't really look.'

Without warning, Mam sprang forward, her arm like a lizard's tongue darting out for a fly, and slapped me hard across the head. 'Stop acting like a pig! How many times do I have to tell you about using a knife and fork?' she growled.

I pressed my lips together, careful not to show how much the blow stung, especially with Keith and Jack sitting opposite. They flinch every time she lays one on me.

Darryl placed the steaming plate of meatballs and creamed potatoes we'd all enjoyed at the spare setting and told Mam to sit down but the disgusted look she gave the food was enough for him to know she wouldn't be touching it. 'Are you being funny? You know I'm not doing carbs! I thought you said you'd do something healthy like a salad?' she complained.

Darryl sighed. 'I've made salads all week. We can't live just on rabbit food, can we?'

Mam stared pointedly at Darryl's belly. 'No, apparently not,' she said coldly. 'Anyway, it doesn't matter. I'll get something down town.'

'Down town?'

'Yeah. I'm going out with Mandy and Risa.'

'Again?' Darryl asked. It was the third time this week she'd been out with those two. She knew them from when she worked on a cruise ship when I was little. I'd had to live with my Nana Lynne and Grandad Martin, Mam's step-dad, back then. It wasn't what you'd call a good experience. Counsellor-lady told me a lot of my 'anger issues' stemmed from that time because I felt I had been abandoned but you don't want to know about stuff like that. I'm over it. End of.

Mam was getting herself really wound up. 'What do you mean "again"?' she snarled, watching Darryl as he took her plate away and scraped the food into the bin. 'What am I? A prisoner in my own home? And it is *my* home, remember. It's *my* name on the papers.'

'So you keep telling me,' Darryl muttered.

Mam seemed to expand then, like an airbed being pumped up. 'Oh, I do, do I? Well, just you listen to me, mate, because . . .'

It had started. I nodded at Jack and Keith and led them out of the kitchen and headed upstairs to my bedroom. 'OK, mushes,' I said, grabbing my football and bouncing it on the floor to try to drown out the shouting, 'who wants a story?'

'I do!' said Jack, jumping on to my bed.

'What about?'

'About when we go to Neverland and meet Peter Pan and the Lost Boys.'

I rolled my eyes at Keith who did the same in return. Neverland stories were all Jack ever asked for. Downstairs, a door banged and something smashed, making both lads shudder. I bounced my football harder and began my story. 'OK. One day in Neverland, Wendy, wearing her new Sunderland shirt . . .'

Chapter Three

Grandad Jake, Kiersten, and Brody arrived at teatime on Sunday to take us back to Wakefield with them. It was a tight fit getting six of us into Grandad Jake's car, top of the range, as Keith pointed out, or not. 'Don't do anything I wouldn't do,' I told Mam and Darryl as they stood stiffly by the kerbside to see us off. They'd barely spoken since the row on Friday night.

'Just make sure you mind your manners,' Mam said to me, flicking her eyes quickly at Kiersten.

'Course I will,' I said, doing a fake burp that made everyone inside the car laugh.

Darryl stepped forward and leaned in close to my side, his face a mixture of concern and unease. 'Look after the lads for me, Jolene, won't you?'

'How can you even ask me that?' I said. 'You know I will.'

He nodded briefly. 'You've got your mobile with you, pet, haven't you?'

'Yep. And Jack's *Peter Pan* DVD and Keith's *Fastcars Monthly*. All the basics.'

'Right then. Give us a call when you get there.'

'We will.'

Mam then muttered something about not having time to hang around all day and retreated into the house. Darryl didn't though. He stayed right on that kerbside, waving at us until we were out of sight. 'He'll be there when we get back, I bet,' I joked.

'I hope so,' Keith whispered.

Keith hardly said a word throughout the journey and neither did Jack. I don't know whether they were quiet because they were still overawed by the company or because they were already missing Darryl but I made up for it by chatting non-stop to Brody about After School club. I wanted to be filled in with *all* the details and launched straight in. 'So what's the theme?'

She flicked her long, curly red hair back and grinned. 'How did I guess this would be your first topic of conversation? OK, the theme is Scrapyard Sculptures. Mrs Fryston's been collecting a whole heap of junk for weeks now to make them. The entire mobile's like some kind of yard sale. I'm totally amazed nobody's broken their neck yet.'

'Oh,' I said. Last time it had been football and other outdoor games; much more up my street. But—you know—whatever.

'And you're sure Alex is going to be there?' I continued. Alex McCormack is one of the kids I met there. She's my best friend.

Brody nodded. 'For sure. She can't wait to see you. And you guys,' she added, smiling at Keith and Jack. They just stared back at her.

'Hey, I hope you lads aren't this quiet all week, you know. I'm relying on you to give me a bit of male support!' Grandad told them.

'They won't be quiet,' I said, 'don't you worry.'

Still, it wasn't until we had said goodnight to everyone and closed the door of the grand bedroom we were sharing, that the lads found their tongues again. Then they began talking over each other in excited whispers. 'This is the best house ever! It's like Mr and Mrs Darling's house in *Peter Pan* but even bigger!' Jack giggled.

'Why are the walls covered in wood and not wallpaper?' Keith asked, passing his hand across the oak panelling. 'And why . . .'

He started asking about everything he'd seen since we arrived. That's what Keith does; you think he's staring into space but he isn't. He never misses a thing; just stores everything up in his brain for when he needs it. I answered him best I could, but not being an expert on big houses, I made half of it up.

'It's all frightfully delightful!' Jack said, unloading his stuffed animals and arranging them across his pillow in this particular order he has. 'Jolene, I think you'd better make tonight's story extra special.'

'And include wooden walls,' Keith said, pulling his pyjamas on.

'Will do,' I said, thinking what I wouldn't be doing was including the words 'frightfully delightful'. Honest—I would have to get Jack off that Peter Pan and Wendy rubbish when we got back, I really would.

Chapter Four

We didn't arrive at After School club until really late the next morning. That was all Brody's fault. She took years to eat her pancakes during breakfast then years more to get dressed. If I didn't know better I'd have said she was dragging it out on purpose.

Finally, at well after ten, we pulled up outside the school gates. The first thing I noticed was they'd been changed. There was new metal fencing all around the entrance and a mean-looking steel gate in place of the old wooden one. 'The school's had a lot of break-ins lately,' Brody said when I mentioned it.

'Same near us,' I told her.

'It's nothing compared to our house, though; it's like a fortress since we got burgled. Did you notice? Lights, cameras, beams, alarms—the works! I mean, I know I was kind of shaken by it at the time but Jake went a little bit OTT if you ask me. Even the rabbit's got a panic button!'

Inside the barriers, though, it was all so familiar and my heart leapt. We're here! I thought. Bring it on! I quickened my pace as we crossed the school playground, leading the way round the back of the red-brick school to the edge of the field where I knew we'd find the After School club. 'It's smaller than I thought it would be,' Keith said as we approached the steps.

'Small is beautiful,' I quipped, leading the way.

Inside, Jack and Keith went back to being a pair of shy Marys, hiding behind me while Kiersten and Brody sorted out admission slips with Mrs Fryston. I didn't protest about Jack and Keith using me as a shield too much. I was feeling a bit shy myself, not that I'd ever admit it in public.

It was a lot busier than last time I'd been. The

place was heaving with kids of all ages, shapes, sizes, and colours but I didn't recognize any of them. Alex certainly wasn't there, though her mam, one of the several helpers, was. Mrs McCormack was looking slightly hassled, as always, as she mopped up a spilt pot of paint from her crowded craft table by the window.

I knew Alex sometimes came later in the holidays depending on what time her sister Caitlin brought her so I tried not to worry too much but it was weird that I didn't know *anyone*. Lloyd or Reggie, Brody's boyfriend, or my old enemy Sammie Wesley or that Sam kid who sometimes spoke in rhymes or even little Brandon, who only missed if there was an emergency. Not one of them was here. I felt the first stab of uncertainty since we arrived. What if they'd all left and After School club was rubbish now?

'It's a bit noisy,' Jack whispered, clinging to my hand.

'And that's before our Keith gets going!' I joked, nudging the silent figure at my side.

He looked lost and ready to do a runner, but then Mrs Fryston saw the three of us and smiled broadly. 'Hello, Jolene. Welcome back. Goodness, you've shot up!' she said.

'People keep telling me that!' I replied.

'And this is Keith and Jack?' she asked, coming over and kneeling down so she was eye level with them.

They stared numbly back at her from behind me. 'Yeah. They're a bit quiet, like, but they'll join in when they're ready.'

'Perhaps they'd like to have a walk round with me, so I can show them what we're doing today?' Mrs Fryston suggested.

I expected them to shake their heads and refuse but I'd forgotten how everyone trusts Mrs Fryston from the start. They disappeared then, over to the far side of the mobile which had been sectioned off with bookcases.

'Well, that's them sorted, what do you want to do?' Brody asked, coming to stand next to me after she'd waved goodbye to Kiersten.

'I don't know,' I said, shrugging my shoulders. 'What is there?'

She stretched her arms out and did this massive yawn. 'Ooh, I don't know about you but I could do with some fresh air. That early start has kind of knocked me out. Do you wanna take a walk round the Patch?'

'The Patch?'

'It's a new thing—a joint venture the school and the After School club are working on. You know where the caretaker's bungalow used to be?'

I nodded, though I didn't really.

'Well, she's been upgraded to a more modern place and they've knocked the old bungalow down and used the land for a kind of wildlife area known as The Patch. It's where we're going to put all the sculptures when they're finished. Come on, I'll show you.'

'OK,' I said, following Brody out reluctantly. The Patch. It sounded well boring.

Chapter Five

At the far end of the field behind the school and what felt like miles across from the mobile

was another fenced-in area. The fencing was quite high—reaching the top of my head—but instead of being  made of wire mesh, this time it was made of long, slanted thick twigs you couldn't see through. 'Willow,' Brody said, stepping through a gate at the side, 'isn't it lovely?'

'If you say so,' I mumbled.

Inside wasn't that much to write home about, either. Just a big square area the size of a tennis court filled with lots of puny-looking plants propped up with bamboo canes. Down the centre ran a winding pathway leading to what looked like a tepee made out of more twigs. The tepee-thing dominated the area, rising high above everything, including the fence, but it still didn't impress me much.

'It's a work in progress,' Brody said, seeing my long face. 'In a couple of years there'll be trees and all kinds of plants in here and maybe a pond. It's a shame I shan't be around to see it. Wanna go sit in the den?'

'Not really,' I said glumly, 'I'd rather go check on our Keith and Jack.'

'Oh, they'll be fine. Come on.' Brody grabbed my hand and pulled me along the path towards the 'den'. 'The Year Sixes at the school built it,' she said, her voice getting louder as we approached the heap, 'some feat of engineering, huh?'

'Mm,' I said, unconvinced.

'Try the door; it's really clever. They've made like a latch so it opens and closes properly. I think Sam and Sammie worked on that part.'

'Great,' I said, flicking up a nub of varnished wood that jutted from a roughly sawn hole in the door. The door, which only came chest high, sprang open instantly, revealing nothing but darkness.

'Go in,' Brody urged.

'OK,' I sighed, crouching and thinking 'what for?' but as soon as I set foot inside I got a right shock. There were yells of 'surprise!' and what felt like dozens of hands grabbing hold of me.

'Jo-lene, Jo-lene, Jo-lene, Jo-le-e-ene!' everyone sang, almost in tune, to the song my name came from. I still couldn't make out who was there but light suddenly appeared as someone rolled up what must have been a blind to reveal a kind of window—if you can call it that, the frame was pretty wonky—and there they all were. Reggie in his goofy specs, Sam Riley with his tidy, blond hair, chunky Sammie Wesley grinning like a cat, little Brandon, dressed in his army combats, Lloyd looking scruffy in his muddy jeans and baggy jumper, and, of course, Alex. Alex, her chestnut hair shining as the sun caught it from behind, had this huge grin on her face and I knew that grin was just for me. One by one they all let go except for her. 'Hello,' Alex said, still squeezing the life out of me, 'what took you?'

Poor Darryl couldn't get a word in edgeways when he phoned that night. The three of us kept passing the phone from one to the other, each telling him something of the day while another one added bits from behind. 'And I played with Brandon nearly all the time,' Jack said. 'He's funny, like Tootles.'

'Tell him about Ruby trying to give the hamster a high-five with her Barbie doll,' Keith whispered.

'And tell him about the trip tomorrow,' I added to that.

Tomorrow, to kick off the summer theme of 'Scrapyard Sculptures' Mrs Fryston had organized a coach to take us to a place called the Yorkshire Sculpture Park which was just outside Wakefield. Apparently it was full of all these sculptures and works of art from famous people dotted about in the open.

'Dad wants to talk to you now,' Jack said, handing the phone over to me.

'About time! You've hogged it for long enough!' I told him. He stuck his tongue out and went to join Keith and Brody in the living room. 'Haway, Darryl, how are you?' I asked.

'I'm fine, pet, and I can tell from your voice and the lads that you all are, too.'

'Oh, yeah. They're loving it!'

'That's good to know, good to know.'

His voice sounded relieved but a bit flat, too. 'What about at home? How's it going with Mam? Is she there? Can I talk to her?'

'Oh, er . . . she's not in at the minute.'

'Don't tell me she's out again.'

'I don't know where she is, to be honest.'

'Well, when she gets back will you tell her I said hello.'

He hesitated for ages before replying. 'Sure I will. Listen, look after the lads for me, won't you?'

'Will you stop asking me that? I told you when we left I'd look after them, didn't I? Flipping heck, man!'

He laughed then, thank goodness. 'Goodnight, Jolene, pet. Sleep tight.'

'You too.'

Aw. I don't want to sound all mushy, but you've got to admit Darryl's just the perfect dad, isn't he?

Chapter Six

Next morning, Kiersten dropped us off in the car park. Brody wasn't with us because she needed to pack for her holidays so Kiersten said she'd wait with us until the coach arrived if we wanted but there was no need. As soon as we got there, Jack and Keith disappeared to be with their mates and I settled down to be with mine, Alex. 'You're like a bunch of old timers,' Kiersten smiled as she drove away.

When the coach came, everyone cheered but no one was allowed on until Mrs Fryston had registered us and done a triple head count and

given everyone a lecture about best behaviour and sticking with our group leaders. There were about twenty-five kids and eight leaders, including Caitlin, Alex's sister, who is one of the holiday staff, and her boyfriend Simon. Jack, Brandon, Ruby, Alex, and me were in Mrs Fryston's group. Keith had joined Lloyd and Reggie and Sam in Caitlin's. Alex was a bit grumpy because she wanted us to be with Caitlin but I pointed out I had to stick with Jack anyway so she was OK then.

The journey only took about forty minutes. I couldn't believe it when Alex told me we were already there. Usually I'm halfway through my lunch by the time I reach my destination on a school trip but I hadn't even had a chance to open my sandwiches before the coach was turning into a gateway bounded by a low drystone wall and signposted 'Yorkshire Sculpture Park'.

'This is it,' Alex said as the coach trundled slowly down a narrow winding road with hills and trees stretching into the distance. Scattered about the fields were all sorts of sculptures: black marble women with holes through their heads; tall, thin metal contraptions; and squat, round objects big enough to climb through. Nothing struck me as being as impressive as the Angel of the North up near us in Gateshead, though. They'd have to go some to beat that. I mean, even my new school had been named after it.

When we jumped down from the coach, Mrs Fryston gave one member from each group a disposable camera so we could take pictures of the sculptures. Alex was in charge of ours and took loads of our favourite: a tall bloke with his arms by his sides painted in a streaky orange. 'Tango Man' we called him.

When we all met up for lunch, Reggie got told off because he'd used all his group's film up on taking snaps of cowpats and sheep droppings and, for once, the others complained about him. When Mrs Fryston asked him why, Reggie just shrugged. 'If that bloke can get away with sawing a shark in half, then a cowpat's a work of art in my book,' he said.

Quick as a flash, our Keith replied, 'That's one book I won't be getting out of the library!' I felt dead proud of him for making everybody laugh. I couldn't wait to tell Darryl how well Keith and Jack were settling in but when Kiersten picked us up she said he'd called already to let us know he had to work overtime and wouldn't be home until after our bedtime. Never mind, I thought, it will keep.

Do you know, I slept like a log that night because of all that fresh air—no, two logs—no, three!

Chapter Seven

Wednesday already—the week was racing away. Today, we actually got down to planning and designing our sculptures that would eventually end up on display in the Patch. Pity I wouldn't be around to see that part but at least I could make a start.

Jack wanted to make his sculpture with Brandon and Keith wanted to do one with Lloyd. All that was fine by me. A: it meant they were settling in, B: it meant I could have some one-on-one time with Alex. We found ourselves a place to work away from everyone else so we could have some peace. 'Did I show you this?' Alex said, sliding a flat brown paper bag towards me.

'What is it?'

'Have a look. I bought it in the shop yesterday.'

I slid out the postcard, which was a picture of that orange sculpture we'd both liked. 'Tango Man!' I said.

'Yeah, but look who it's by.'

I flipped over to read the writing. '"One and Other" by Antony Gormley! He did the Angel of the North! No wonder we liked this one best. He's the man, he is.'

Alex grinned and pulled me over to the window. 'Look what I baggied last night when everybody had gone home,' she whispered, and pulled the curtain back to show me an old tailor's dummy.

'Perfect!' I said.

'Except the head's missing.'

'No problem. We don't want to copy Tango Man exactly, do we? We'll call it . . . Headless Herbert.'

'And paint it yellow instead of orange.'

'Exactly.'

'Let's get going then!' she said.

We spent all day covering Headless Herbert in mod rock so the paint wouldn't just sink into the fabric. That was Alex's idea; she's clever like that. It was really good, too; everyone who passed told us so.

While we made our sculpture, Alex and I just talked and talked, not even bothering to stop for lunch. It was as if we knew we had to get a term's worth of nattering in before I went back to Washington. We talked about ordinary stuff, like how I felt about moving to a new school and how she felt about going into Year Six. She said she was worried about doing the SATs and I told her not to be because they were a piece of cake. When we were sure no one was listening, we got more personal. I asked her what was happening with her brother Daniel's grave. He was only four when he died and his ashes have been stuck on their mantelpiece for, like, twelve years or something, but they were getting a proper grave now. 'It's all arranged,' Alex said, 'the headstone's nearly ready and we're going to have a family service for him in early August. The nice thing is he'll be quite close to Grandma's plot.'

'That's mint,' I said, 'he'll have someone to talk to.'

'Yeah.' She took another layer of mod rock and soaked it in water. 'I'll miss him, though. Is that weird, do you think? Missing someone's ashes?'

'No. Why is it? I mean, it's still your brother, isn't it? I'd be just the same if anything happened to Keith or Jack.'

'Would you?'

'Course.'

'That's nice. It shows how much you love them, even though they're not your real brothers, if you know what I mean.'

'Yeah, I do know what you mean but I don't see what difference that makes. I know loads of people with real brothers and they hate their guts.'

'That's true!' Alex laughed.

I glanced round quickly, to check my lads were OK. Jack was sticking a kitchen roll tube to a cardboard box, concentrating so hard his tongue was sticking out. Keith was hunched over a large sheet of paper, pointing things out to Lloyd who nodded and then bent to add something with his pencil. Keith must have felt me staring at him then because he looked up and smiled. I stuck my thumb up at him and winked. No, if anything happened to either Keith or Jack, I'd be gutted.

'Will they go to the same high school as you when they're old enough?' Alex asked. 'I'm going to the same one as Caitlin.'

'Yeah, I hope so. Eh, did I tell you about the sports facilities?'

'Yeah, about a million times.'

'What, even the all-weather pitch?'

'Two million times.'

I laughed and so did she. For some reason, we kept laughing, and couldn't stop. My stomach was killing me in the end. When Mrs

Fryston came across to see what the racket was, she shook her head and smiled. 'That's what I like to see. Best friends having a good time.'

Chapter Eight

After the club had finished, Grandad Jake picked us up and drove straight to Piccollino's, an Italian restaurant near the station where I'd been before. Brody and Kiersten were already waiting outside, sussing out the specials on the blackboard. 'I just didn't feel like cooking,' Kiersten explained as she pushed open the glass door to go in. 'Besides, I'm trying to run the fridge down. I don't want things rotting in there while we're away.' They were travelling to Heathrow first thing Saturday morning, so it made sense.

It was fun, that meal. I was so chilled out from

being with Alex all afternoon I didn't have much more to say. That didn't matter, though. I was happy just watching and listening to everyone else. Brody made us all laugh by talking about her aunties in Topeka they would be staying with and how 'ditzy' they all were. Jack made *me* laugh by just staring at Brody, all goofy, as she talked. I think Reggie had better watch out—he had competition there. Keith surprised me the most, waving his arms about all over the place at us about his sculpture and how he and Lloyd had spent most of their time walking round the Patch, working out where would be the best position for it. 'We thought next to the den but then it won't catch the light there so we're now thinking near the fence so it gets a striped effect when the sun shines on it.'

'That's real artistic thinking,' Kiersten complimented him.

'Oh,' he said, blushing.

'Well, Keith, laddo, you've certainly bucked up since you arrived!' Grandad told him which is just what I'd been thinking. I wasn't the only one who changed when they got to Brody's After School club.

We were all full after the main course and none of us wanted a pudding so we were back at the house by half past seven. Brody put her new CD on and we were all singing along to that when we pulled into the drive.

'Whose is that?' Grandad asked as he had to pull up behind a car blocking his way. 'Are we expecting anyone, Kierst?'

'That's Dad!' Keith announced before she could reply.

Chapter Nine

After the excitement of seeing Darryl on the doorstep, we all went inside but once he'd sat down and I looked at him properly, I knew something was wrong. He looked terrible; he hadn't shaved, his shirt was all creased and not even buttoned up properly, and he couldn't sit still. One second he was leaning back against the cushions on the settee, one leg bouncing up and down restlessly, the next he was hunched forward, his knees pressed into the low coffee table in front of him. I sighed and came right out with it. 'What's Mam done now?' I asked him.

He let out this fake laugh and said, 'Oh, nothing, nothing.'

Like I believed that.

I got up and planted myself right in front of him, folding my arms across my chest so he knew I meant business. 'What's going on, Darryl? Tell me,' I said.

'Jolene,' Grandad said, 'let the poor guy have his tea.'

'It's all right, Jake, Jolene's right, something's cropped up,' Darryl replied, not looking at me.

'Such as?' I asked, not budging. Bad news is best delivered quick, I reckon.

Darryl cleared his throat a couple of times before answering. 'Well, it's like this,' he began, then stopped, glanced up at me for a second, shook his head and mumbled.

'What?'

'Their nan's sick. She was taken into hospital . . .' he said, trailing off, too cut up to continue.

There was an outbreak of 'oh nos' and 'I'm

sorrys' from everyone, including me. I felt like a proper toe-rag then. There was me acting all bolshy and making Darryl come right out with his bad news in front of everyone when he'd probably been saving it until he had us in private. I liked their nan, too. She was called Pam and she was a warden in an old people's complex and she always let me choose her lottery numbers for her.

'What's wrong with her?' Keith asked, his eyes brimming with tears. 'Is she going to die?'

'No! No!' Darryl said in alarm, his face turning beetroot. 'But the sooner we set off, the sooner we get to see her, yeah?'

Keith nodded and took Jack's hand. 'We'll go get our stuff,' he said, his voice all choked.

'Yeah,' I said, patting Darryl on the shoulder before I went, 'we won't be long.' It was a bummer I'd miss out on the last two days with Alex and wouldn't get to finish Headless Herbert with her but family comes first, right?

I turned to follow Jack and Keith upstairs but Darryl stood up then, nearly sending all the tea things flying. 'Jolene, no,' he said, his voice low but sharp, 'it's just the lads. You stay here. Your mam's coming for you on Friday as planned. No point you cutting your holiday short, is there?'

'But I want to . . .'

'Please, pet,' he said, more softly this time, 'it's less complicated this way.'

Chapter Ten

Next day felt funny without Jack and Keith at
After School club. Everyone was sympathetic but
Lloyd and Brandon were the most disappointed.
'Oh, but I needed Keith to choose the final design
for our sculpture,' Lloyd said, scratching the back
of his neck.

'I'll ask him tonight when I talk to him,' I
promised.

'Jack was going to play with me,' Brandon
pouted.

'I'll tell him you asked after him when I phone,'
I promised again.

Trouble was, nobody answered when I called the house. The phone just rang and rang. Neither Darryl or Mam returned my texts, either, but Grandad Jake told me he didn't think mobile phones were allowed to be switched on in hospital wards. They mess up the heart monitors or something.

It was about half nine when Mam finally picked up the phone at home. 'Hello?' she answered, her voice all croaky and choked up.

'Hi, it's me,' I said.

'Oh, Jolene,' she sobbed.

'What's wrong? Is it Pam?'

'What?'

'Pam. Is it bad?'

'What are you talking about?'

'P-a-m. Pam, Darryl's mam. The one that's really ill in hospital, remember!'

'Oh, that's what he told you, is it?' She laughed but it turned into a snort then another sob.

'What do you mean?' I asked.

Mam took a deep breath. 'He's left me, Jolene. He's left me—wants a divorce as soon as possible.'

I suppose I should have felt shocked but I didn't. The news wasn't exactly unexpected. How could it be, the way they'd been hammering on when I left? Mam went on and on about what a useless husband Darryl had been, especially after all she had done for him. 'How dare he leave me, the big lump!' she ended.

'I've no idea, Mam. It's a mystery,' I said, then checked what time she'd be coming for me.

'Mid-morning and you'd better be ready. I've got to work late.'

'Great,' I said and hung up.

Being picked up mid-morning meant I didn't have time to go to After School club the next day. I called Alex's house first thing and told her why. 'Oh, Jolene, I'm really sorry,' she said, sounding all upset.

'Forget it,' I replied, 'I'm not bothered. It's not

like it's a total shock or anything. Sorry about dumping you with Headless Herbert on your own.'

'It's OK. I'll send you a picture of him when he's finished.'

'That'd be mint.'

There was a pause and I could almost feel her frowning through the telephone wires. 'Are you sure you're OK, Jolene?' she asked.

'What do you mean?'

'It's just you sound way too calm. If my parents had split up I'd be crying my eyes out.'

'Yeah, but your parents actually like each other!'

'I guess. What about Keith and Jack? You're going to really miss them, aren't you?'

'Why?'

She hesitated, thinking she'd said the wrong thing. 'Well . . . er . . . you won't see them as much, will you?'

'Yeah, course I will. I'll be seeing them every day, seeing as I'll be living with them!'

'Oh,' Alex said, sounding surprised, 'I thought you'd be with your mum.'

202

I nearly started choking when she said that. 'Eh? What would I want to live with my mam for? Darryl's much better at bringing kids up—he's a natural. My mam's rubbish—she's the first to admit it. She left me to live with my nan for four years once, remember.'

'I know but she's still your mum . . .' Alex began but I interrupted her. I wanted her to get this straight from the start because living with my mam instead of Darryl was not—repeat *not*—an option. 'Look, who's the one who turns up for Leavers' Services and parents' evenings? Darryl. Who asks me what sort of day I've had and if I'm OK as soon as I walk in? Darryl. Who never shouts at me or slaps me round the head? Darryl. Do you get what I'm saying or do you want more examples?'

'OK, OK, don't get your knickers in a twist; I was only asking! I just thought your mum might have wanted you to stay with her. She'll be all alone, won't she?'

'Yeah! For about two seconds until she finds a new boyfriend!'

'She might not.'

I was going to laugh but I stopped myself. Alex only saw the good side of people and I didn't want her to think I was being cruel. It's just I knew what Mam was like, that's all. If Alex had been let down by her mam as often as I'd been let down by mine, she'd be reacting the same way as I was now. 'I'll probably see Mam at weekends,' I said instead.

Alex didn't say anything for a few seconds; I could tell she was having trouble taking it all in. Her world and mine were so different sometimes. 'Oh . . . well . . . let me know your new address, won't you?' she said.

'Definitely. I'll let you know it as soon as I find out myself. It probably won't be a massive house or anything but who cares as long as we're together, right?'

'Right! Oh, good luck with everything, Jolene.'

'Ta!'

'I am sorry.'

'Well you don't have to be! It's not your fault,

you daft nit! Anyway, I'd better go. Talk to you
soon, Alex.'

'Hope so.'

'Know so!'

Chapter Eleven

When Mam arrived, all puffy-eyed, she wouldn't even stay for a coffee. 'Can't,' she told Grandad Jake when he asked, 'I get too weepy when I just sit—I need to be on the move and doing things.' It didn't stop her sneaking a long look at what Kiersten was wearing from under her eyelids when she thought no one was watching, though. You see, I know what she's like. Those tears would dry up faster than a puddle in a desert as soon as we got outside.

I was glad Mam wanted a quick getaway, though. I don't like long goodbyes, either, and the sooner we got home, the sooner I could start packing. Brody nearly crushed my ribs with her hug and said she was missing me already, Grandad handed me twenty pounds for 'things' for my new school, and Kiersten said that I was welcome to stay with them any time. 'She's been adorable,' she told Mam.

Mam frowned. 'Adorable? Our Jolene?'

In the car, Mam did nothing but moan all the way to the motorway. 'So, they're off to America for a month in the morning. Huh! It's all right for some.' It was no use telling Mam it wasn't really a holiday, just a long round of visiting relatives. I leaned forward to switch on the radio but she told me to switch it off again. 'I've got a headache,' she said. 'Anyway, I want to talk to you.'

'What about?'

'What about? The weather, of course! Honestly!

What do you think about?' she snapped, pulling into the outside lane of the A1 carriageway to overtake a row of northbound lorries.

'OK,' I said, 'talk.'

After all that she didn't say anything for a minute, just kept on overtaking in the outside lane, a deep scowl on her face. Eventually, she glanced sideways at me, biting her lip. 'Jolene, I'm going to be straight with you because that's how you and me are, right? Straight with each other? No beating about the bush?'

'I suppose.'

'Well, now Darryl's gone, things are going to get a bit tight financially . . .'

'Mmm.'

'And while I love my job it doesn't pay enough

to keep the mortgage going on my own but there's no way I'm selling my house.'

'OK.'

'That's our future in that house and I've worked my fingers to the bone for it.'

'OK,' I said, hoping the whole conversation wasn't going to be as boring as this. Mam took a deep breath and came to the point.

'Well . . . there's a job going . . .'

'Yeah?'

'. . . on the *Belle Helene* . . .'

'Mandy's boat?'

She nodded and began talking really fast as if her life depended upon it. 'The Tropical Paradise Tour. I'm thinking about applying but I wanted to run it by you first. See how you felt. It'd only be six months away but . . . it means I could rent the house out and that would sort the mortgage for a bit . . . plus I'd be earning. You get amazing tips on the cruises; so many rich old biddies wanting treatments and paying top whack for them . . .'

'Go for it,' I said.

She almost steered into the crash barrier when she heard that. 'Really?'

'Yeah, why not?'

'I thought you'd be mad at me.'

'Why should I be?'

She laughed nervously. 'Well, it'd mean you living with Nana and Grandad Martin and going to a different high school.'

I laughed then. 'Yeah, as if!'

'What do you mean "as if"?'

'As if I'll be at Nana's when I'll be with Darryl.'

'Eh? No you won't.'

'Course I will.'

She gave an empty, howling laugh then when she realized I was being serious. 'So that's why you've been so laid-back about everything? You think you're going to live with that big lump?'

'He's called Darryl,' I said through gritted teeth.

'Well, think again! He won't have you.'

'Yeah, whatever.'

Mam concentrated on the road for a minute, a deep scowl on her face. 'I'm telling you for a fact he won't.'

'Whatever.'

She glanced at me, her face set hard. 'Well, that's brilliant, that is! That makes me feel wonderful. Here I am, heartbroken, looking for a bit of support and what do I get? My own daughter doesn't even want to live with me. She just instantly presumes she's going to live with some bloke she's not even related to.'

'He's not some bloke. You were married to him!'

'So?'

'So talk sense.'

Mam was getting madder and madder. 'Don't tell me to talk sense! Ooh! I knew you'd come back from that place full of it.'

I sighed. I didn't want an argument about Grandad and Kiersten. I just wanted to get back to Washington. 'I don't get why you're kicking up a fuss about me living with Darryl. You've just told me I won't *be* living with you, haven't you? You'll be in a tropical paradise, so what difference does it make?'

Mam took her left hand off the steering wheel

and slammed me so hard I'd have dinted the door if I hadn't been wearing a seatbelt. 'How many more times?' she yelled at me. 'He won't have you! I wish he would! You deserve each other!'

'All you have to do is drop me off there!' I bellowed right back at her.

'Fine,' Mam snarled, pushing her foot down on the accelerator, 'I'll drop you off there. Let's see what happens, shall we?'

'Yeah,' I said, looking straight ahead, my hands shaking from the argument, 'let's.'

Chapter Twelve

Neither of us spoke again until we were on the outskirts of Washington, when Mam turned right on to the Armstrong Industrial estate, then did an emergency stop outside Crossley and Singh's, the big do-it-yourself store and builder's merchants where Darryl worked. 'Right then,' she said.

'Right then what?'

'You don't believe me? Go ask him for yourself. Go on, go ask him.'

I frowned at her but she just pulled down the vanity

mirror in the car sunshield and began to put lipstick on.

'Now? I don't want to now,' I said, less certain than I had been. The long silence had given me time to think; time to wonder why Darryl hadn't just taken me back with him the other day when he'd picked up the lads. Time to admit Mam might just be telling the truth and that he actually didn't want me. Mam might be a lot of things but she didn't usually lie about stuff. 'He might not be there,' I said, trying not to show how uncertain I felt.

'He'll be there and I'll be here. Waiting.'

She said it so cockily I wanted to knock the lipstick out of her hand and scribble over her silly face with it. 'Don't bother,' I told her, snatching my backpack instead, 'I'll probably go straight home with him.'

'I'll wait all the same,' she said.

'Please yourself,' I told her, leaping out of the car. If she wanted to waste her time, that was up to her.

I hurried through the automatic glass entrance door but I knew I wouldn't be allowed to continue through into the loading bays so I had to ask the bloke on the help desk to send out a message over the tannoy system for Darryl. I felt dead important when they announced 'Will Darryl Birtley please report to the enquiries desk as he has a visitor.'

Darryl, wearing a tangerine coloured boiler-suit and wiping his hands on a grimy cloth, approached the desk with a puzzled look on his face. When he saw me, the look changed to confusion. 'Haway, pet. What are you doing here? You're not alone, are you?' he asked nervously, looking round.

I couldn't answer at first, I was just so pleased to see him. Forgetting all the nasty things Mam had said, I hugged him and told him I'd come straight here after Mam had picked me up from Grandad Jake's. 'Oh,' he said, sounding embarrassed.

I didn't want to make him feel bad by reminding him he'd fibbed about Pam so I rattled on about the journey and Headless Herbert and other rubbish for a few minutes instead. 'Anyway, here

I am, Trouble United! What time do you finish? Shall I just wait for you or what?'

Darryl glanced up at the help desk bloke and steered me towards the display of garden benches nearby. 'What do you mean, pet?'

'Shall I just hang round here—you know—until it's time for you to take me home with you? I can pick up all my clothes and stuff tomorrow. I just want to come back with you and see the lads now.'

A shadow crossed his face. 'I can't take you home with me, Jolene.'

'Why not?' I asked. I tried to keep my voice steady. There'd be a dead simple reason. Overtime, bet you.

He slumped down on one of the benches and I slumped next to him. 'Well, I haven't got a home, to start with. The lads are at their mam's and I'm at my mam's until I get sorted out.'

I let this news sink in for a second. It wasn't great news but it wasn't a disaster, was it? Darryl hadn't said he didn't want me, only that things were tough at the moment. 'How long do you think it'll be until you are sorted?' I asked him.

He ran his hand roughly over his prickly hair. 'Weeks, months, who knows? It depends on what the solicitors have to say . . . I saw them this morning . . . it wasn't . . .'

'Wasn't what?' I asked him when he didn't finish his sentence.

He looked at me, then quickly looked at his feet, shaking his head. 'It wasn't good.'

I shrugged. Solicitors didn't mean much to me; I didn't know or care what they did. All I needed to know, really, really needed to know, was when I could move in with Darryl. I leaned over and nudged his arm, looking up at the ceiling as if to say, 'What a pain, eh?'

'I suppose I could go back to Mam's for a bit but try and get fixed up before I start at the Angel, won't you, mush? I don't want to miss the trials for the girls' footy team.' I said it in a light, jokey way but he knew I meant it.

All the colour drained from Darryl's face but he just shook his head. 'Jolene, you can't live with me, pet, not ever.'

I gave him a wonky smile. I hadn't heard him properly. 'What?'

'You can't live with me . . . with us. I'm not . . . I'm not your proper dad.'

Well, we all knew that. My so-called 'proper' dad had done a runner before I'd even been born. What had that got to do with it? I laughed. It came out sounding fake, even to me. 'So? Who cares about that? You're like a proper dad so that's all that matters, isn't it? It's like I said to Alex the other day when she was talking about Jack and Keith not being my real brothers . . .'

I repeated the conversation I'd had with Alex and waited for him to nod and say, 'Course it is, pet. I don't know what I'm on about!' But he didn't. He just began shaking his head as he backed up to the corner of the bench, away from me. 'No,' he said, 'no, no, no. Don't do this to me, pet. I'm worried enough about having to leave Jack and Keith with Tracie. It took me that long to get custody of them in the first place. I can't worry about you, too.'

I stared at him for a minute, thinking why?

Why couldn't he worry about me too? Because if he didn't worry about me, it meant Mam hadn't been telling fibs in the car. It meant he didn't want me. And if he didn't want me, it would break my heart. 'Darryl,' I said, reaching out my hand to touch him, but he jumped up as if he'd spilt hot tea down his overalls.

'No, Jolene,' he said, wincing, 'I can't do this. Go home. Go to your mam.'

And he stalked off without looking back at all. The big lump.

Mam took one look at my face as I flung myself into the front seat next to her and twisted the key in the ignition with a flourish. 'Told you,' she said.

Chapter Thirteen

I stayed in my bedroom all weekend, barring the door and screaming at Mam to bleep-bleep off every time she came near. 'Suit yourself, Jolene,' she said in the end, 'I've got better things to do than waste time on your moods.'

On Saturday night, when I knew Mam was asleep, I sneaked downstairs to get something to eat. 'Like a midnight feast in Neverland,' I imagined Jack whispering. Jack and Keith. Where were they tonight? I wondered what fibs Darryl had told *them* on the journey home? Did they know they wouldn't be living with me again?

Would maybe never see me again? Because that's what happened. I'd talked to enough kids at school whose parents had split to know the score. It started off with weekend visits, if you were lucky, then every other weekend, then now and again in the holidays, then maybe some other time . . . then nothing. Huh! I hadn't even started off with weekend visits, had I? I'd gone straight to nothing.

I opened the fridge door but instead of seeing cheese and salad, I just saw Darryl's stupid face. 'I'm not your proper dad. I can't worry about *you*, Jolene!' it sneered. I slammed the fridge door shut and dashed back upstairs.

I didn't think of a comeback until I was on the dark landing. *Well, just because you don't want me, it doesn't mean the lads don't!*

Yeah, Dad. Just because you don't want her doesn't mean we don't! their voices echoed in support.

I stopped by their old bedroom, laying my head on the smooth paintwork for a second. I missed them so much already. Turning the handle carefully so Mam wouldn't wake, I tiptoed into their room, just to feel nearer to them. Maybe I'd sleep on one of their beds, or maybe I'd find something of theirs I could keep under my pillow, as a memento.

It was a mistake, going in there. A big mistake. Even though I hadn't turned on the light, the moon was shining so clearly through the curtainless window, what I saw really shocked and hurt me, like a mis-kicked ball in the guts or one of Mam's unexpected back-handers. Smack—take that!

Their room had been stripped bare. All their furniture, curtains, toys, games, everything. There wasn't even a pair of socks left to remind me who'd once lived here. Not a thing. Mam had scrubbed Jack and Keith out of her life just like Darryl had scrubbed me out of his.

Grown-ups. They made me sick.

I spent the rest of the night staring out of my bedroom window, trying to send signals to Jack and Keith miles away at their mam's, wherever that was, to let them know I wouldn't forget them, ever.

'Do you want a story?' I whispered.

Chapter Fourteen

On Monday morning, Mam rapped sharply on my door and told me she was going to work. 'I want you up and dressed by the time I come home or else, Jolene! Enough is enough!'

She was right. Enough was enough and I'd *had* enough—of her, of Darryl, of the lot of them. The second I heard her car roar away, I threw back my duvet, headed for the bathroom, took a shower, had a sniff at my Sunderland shirt and decided it was minging, chucked it in the laundry basket and put on my clean replica away-shirt instead.

Downstairs, I made a pot of tea and some toast. My backpack was still on the chair where I'd flung it, unopened. That was good—it would save a bit of time on the packing. I began rummaging about in the fridge; I'd need food to take with me. Kiersten had said she was trying to get rid of all her fresh food. No point arriving at Grandad Jake's with nothing to eat. That'd be daft.

Back to Grandad Jake's; that's where I was going today. I wasn't going to hang around here until Mam decided to bunk off on her cruise ships. I knew her. Six months would turn into six years; she'd done it before and she'd do it again. Well, stuff that for a game of soldiers. I wasn't going to live with Nana Lynne and Grandad Martin again. She was always sozzled and he was always nasty. I'd have no arms left by the time he'd finished pinching and nipping them. Stay with them, Mam? You're having a laugh.

I'd go to the one place I've always been made to feel welcome. What was it Kiersten had said before I left? You're welcome here any time, Jolene? Well, any time had come. All I had to do was lie low for a month until they returned from Topeka.

It was a cinch getting on the train at Newcastle. I just told the woman at the counter that my dad was parking the car when she asked if I was unaccompanied. Then when she asked why we didn't get our tickets at the same time I thought of Grandad Jake and said, 'Dad's already got a season ticket, he's a commuter,' and that was that. Mission accomplished.

It was only lunchtime, so I found an empty seat easily enough and stared out of the window the whole journey, remembering this time last year. I had run away from home then, too. Mam had arranged to go on holiday without me and I was meant to stay at Grandad Martin and Nana's. No change there, then. I don't know why she always dumped me with them when she knew they were useless and I hated them. 'They're the only ones that will have you,' she always said when I asked her. Was that true? Was that why Darryl had been so quick to get rid of me? I was too much trouble? Get over it, Jolene, I growled to myself. What did I care? I was Jolene Nevin, captain of fights and flare-ups, me. I didn't need anybody.

I crunched into my apple, and planned what to do when I got to Grandad Jake's house. Take a shower in their posh en suite? Make myself some of those golden pancakes Brody loved? Watch a bit of telly? I'd check out the Sunderland website on the Internet, too, to see if we'd bought any new players. Easy life, Jolene, I thought, snuggling right down in my seat. 'Girl, you are a genius!'

It was when I stood outside Kirkham Lodge, three hours later, staring at the electronic gates that were normally open but were now fastened and padlocked, I realized I might not be such a genius after all. I'd forgotten one or two things about what people do when they go on holiday. Things like cancelling the milk and shutting the house up good and proper. At Kirkham Lodge it wasn't like we were talking about making sure the door was locked, either. Brody hadn't been exaggerating that day she told me about the burglar alarms; we really were talking sensors, floodlights, and cameras.

I glanced up at the high sandstone wall on either side of the gates and knew I had no chance of getting into the house. I'd be busted the second I touched the front door, if I even got that far without being electrocuted or something. Bogger. Bogger, bogger, bogger! I hadn't thought this through at all.

Chapter Fifteen

Well, I wasn't going back home, that was
definite. Mam would go mental—probably
phone Grandad Martin straight away and tell him
to bring his belt round. No way was I going back
to that. Besides, I didn't have enough money for
a return fare. I'd used up all my replica shirt
money on the single ticket coming and only
had the twenty quid Grandad had given me
left over.

Instead, I walked back into Wakefield and spent
the rest of the afternoon hanging round the city
centre. Nobody gave me a second glance. It was

the summer holidays, after all, so there were plenty of kids my age roaming round.

I ate some of my biscuits on a bench outside the cathedral, saving the crisps and cheese until later, then I walked round the streets exploring. I found Brody's posh girls' school up near a hospital and then had a quick nosy round an art gallery nearby. I felt dead proud because in three hours I hadn't spent any money and had still kept myself busy. Eventually I was bursting for the loo so I headed for the bus station. I used the facilities, washed my hands in the sink, then filled my water bottle from the tap. I wasn't daft enough to get caught without water, was I? And it was free—double result.

I checked my watch; it was just after six. Mam wouldn't even be home yet and here I was, already a hundred miles away. I thought about sending her a quick text to say I was fine but when I checked my mobile, it was as flat as a pancake because I hadn't recharged it since last week. Never mind, I thought; she couldn't care less anyway.

It was the rush hour now and people were milling

around catching buses home after work. It was then I saw the number thirty-nine which I knew was the one Alex always caught when she went into town. My heart skipped a beat. That was it! I could catch that bus and be outside Alex's house in ten minutes. She'd be back from After School club now and well pleased to see me! I could kip down on her bedroom floor for a few days and . . .

The smile faded. What if her mam answered the door? Or her dad? Or Caitlin? They'd give me a cup of tea then be on the phone to Mam quicker than you could say 'Headless Herbert'. I'd be back to square one. I couldn't risk it. Maybe I could call her from a phone box, though . . . arrange to meet her somewhere . . .

'Are you all right, lovey? You look a bit lost?'

I felt someone tug on my backpack and spun round to see an old geezer staring up at me from a bench. He had a whiskery chin and yellow, broken teeth. Tramp alert! 'I'm not your lovey,' I said, scowling at him to show I meant business.

He took a swig from a plastic cup and shrugged. 'Just askin' that's all. No harm in askin' is there? Why don't you sit here and talk to Old Duggan for two minutes? I could do with some company.' He patted the space next to him.

Not on your nelly, smelly, I thought. I was on the number thirty-nine bus in two seconds flat.

I wasn't sure where to get off so I waited until I recognized Alex's house then got off the stop after that. I knew I was on Zetland Avenue so I cut through a side street. It was still light. I didn't want to stray too far from Alex's but I didn't want to risk bumping into Mrs McCormack or anyone from the club, either. The side street I'd picked came to a dead end, with only a narrow alley down one side and a fenced-in field facing me. A fenced-in field? Yes! It was the school playing field—it had to be! I ran down the alley, knowing now it led to the main entrance to the school.

I was right. One–nil to Nevin. As I ran, the first thing that came into view was the top of the tepee in the Patch. The Patch! I slowed right down then, my heart pounding, as I walked parallel to the dense willow walls only a few metres across from the security fencing. Jolene, lass, I said to myself, you've found yourself a bed for the night.

I knew I'd never be able to climb over the security fence without being caught but luckily I didn't need to. I spied a gap under it where the mesh had buckled because someone or something—dogs probably—had dug beneath it. Luckily the end house adjoining the alley was boarded up and empty, so I knew I wouldn't be spotted by nosy neighbours from that side. Checking no one was around, I pushed my backpack up and through the gap and followed it, hoping digging was all the dogs had done in the hole.

I then pelted the short way towards the perimeter of the Patch, running round the willow fencing until I reached the gate and then, once inside, strode up to the door of the tepee, clicked open the door latch Sam Riley had so carefully designed, and let myself in.

I glanced round, trying to adjust to the gloom.

As far as I could make out, it was just an empty space apart from the beanbags scattered round the base of the tepee.

The ground and lower half of the wall had plastic sheeting to waterproof the place, overlaid with seagrass matting, so it wasn't damp or anything. Still, it wasn't what you'd call cosy either. I sighed. It would have to do for now.

Chapter Sixteen

I slept there that night and the night after that. It was easy, really. I knew Mrs McCormack and Mrs Fryston arrived about half past seven to set up the breakfast club for the early birds. All I did was make sure I was gone by then and creep back into the tepee after seven in the evening. I could carry on doing that for a few weeks until Grandad came home, no problem. I had already decided not to try to contact Alex. It would only put her in an awkward position and I knew what a rubbish fibber she was. Besides, I couldn't be much closer to her, could I? This was nearly as good as actually seeing her.

Funnily enough, it wasn't the night times that bothered me; I've never been scared of the dark or anything. It was the days. I hadn't bargained for how time would drag. Wakefield isn't as big as Sunderland or Newcastle and there isn't that much to do for twelve hours when you're on your own without much money.

On the third day, it rained all the time and I got soaked. I tried to get in to the afternoon showing at the cinema but when I reached the counter, I didn't have enough cash left to pay for a ticket. I'd tried to be careful with Grandad's twenty but a Big Mac here and bus fare there—that was it: I'd run out of money. I was skint already.

I trundled miserably round the Ridings Shopping Centre, slowly drying out but feeling hungrier and hungrier. I needed to sort myself out—fast.

When I woke up on the fourth morning, stiff

and tired, I ached all over and couldn't stop shivering. I closed my eyes, which burnt behind the lids. I forced myself to get up from the middle of the floor and dumped the beanbags I'd slept on back in their place. Today, I reckoned, I'd check out Grandad's house again. There might be a back way I could get in and even his potting sheds had to be better than this. Besides, I'd begun to change my mind about being so close to Alex. What was the point of being so near to her and the After School club when I couldn't see her or join in with anything? Talk about rubbing my nose in it.

I had just pushed the beanbag back into place when I heard a noise. I listened again. There was definitely someone coming up the path—not just one person, either, loads of them. Their footsteps crunched noisily on the gravel. I checked my watch and nearly died on the spot. It was eight o'clock already! What were they doing coming in here, though? It was still early.

I dived under the nearest beanbags for cover, frantically pulling them over me so I just had enough air to breathe. It's a good job I did because seconds later the latch on the tepee door opened and in they came.

'Put the grub in the middle,' I heard Reggie order.

'What about the drinks?' Lloyd asked.

'Same, and wipe your feet on the mat, all of you,' ordered Reggie. Who'd died and made him king? I wondered, poking a tiny hole between the folds of the beanbag so I could breathe better. Oh, I felt totally bunged up. I hoped they wouldn't be long.

There was a lot of shuffling and banging about, then Alex spoke, and I had to force myself to stay still so that I didn't leap out and grab her. 'Shall we sit in a circle? Circles are best for discussions, I think.' Her voice was flat and empty.

'Yeah, whatever,' Reggie agreed.

'I'm going to shove something against the door in case Mrs Fryston comes.' That was bossy Sammie Wesley.

'What did you tell her we were doing?' Reggie asked.

'Planning where to put the sculptures.'

'Nice one,' Reggie said.

There was more shuffling and I realized people were dragging beanbags to the middle to sit on. I grabbed hold of the one covering me and hoped nobody would try to pull it away. My heart was racing but the good thing about having anger-management lessons is you get taught how to breathe, slow and deep, to calm yourself down when you're feeling stressed. Well, I couldn't be any more stressed than this. I concentrated hard on my breathing; in through the nose, out through the mouth, in through the nose, out through the mouth. I didn't relax a muscle until I heard Reggie ask if everybody was ready and I knew my beanbag was safe. There was a chorus of yesses. 'OK, then,' he said, all solemn like the vicar who did our Tuesday assemblies at school, 'who wants to kick off?'

Chapter Seventeen

'I'll start,' I heard Lloyd say. 'I think we've got to work out what we'd do if we were running away. You know, put yourself in Jolene's place.'

My place? This whole meeting was about me? I was all ears now. 'If it were me,' Lloyd continued, 'I'd go down by the canal. There are loads of places to hide there. Even near where I live there's an empty lock-keeper's cottage. It's boarded up but you can get inside easily and it's dry. I've played in there loads of times with my brother Huw and his friends.'

Thanks for the tip, mush, I thought.

'No way!' Alex said in alarm. 'I'd hate it if she went there; it's too creepy and dangerous.'

'Anyway, the police have already searched round the canal,' Sammie Wesley added.

What? The police? What police? I forced my breathing to slow down as much as I could without it actually stopping.

'How do you know that?' Lloyd asked.

'It was on *Calendar News*, dingbat.'

'Well, I didn't know, did I? We don't all have televisions,' Lloyd replied, sounding offended.

'Did you see the interview with her mum? She was crying her eyes out,' Sammie continued in that tone people use when they are pretending to care but really they're just loving the drama.

'What do you expect?' Reggie snapped.

Sammie ignored him. 'I'm just giving Lloyd the details. He needs to know. Anyway, she was twisting Jolene's Sunderland shirt round and round in her hand, going "She'd never have gone without her shirt. If anything's happened to her, I don't know what I'll do; she's all I've got." My mum was in bits then. I had to pass her the tissues.

She said it's a mother's worst nightmare, having one of your kids go missing.'

I didn't know what shocked me most: the idea of Mam appearing on TV or the thought of her wringing my Sunderland shirt. I should never have left it in the wash. Next second, I heard Alex sobbing and Sammie saying sorry and that she didn't mean to upset her. If they'd been giving out medals in willpower right then, I'd have got gold. How I managed to stay beneath that beanbag I'll never know. I felt sweat pouring down my face. I was cold and hot at the same time. There was too much to take in, especially when my head felt as if it was stuffed full of soggy Weetabix.

'Chin up, lass,' Reggie said, 'Jolene's tough, she'll be fine.'

'She's still only eleven,' Alex mumbled, and I could tell from her voice she was trying to hold herself together. 'I'm really worried. Nobody's seen her since Monday and today's Thursday.'

'If it *was* her that eyewitness saw in the bus station on Monday; we can't be sure,' Lloyd said.

What 'eyewitness'? That old geezer?

'I just don't get why she hasn't called Alex if she is in Wakefield like the police think. That's what I'd have done, first thing, called my best mate,' Sammie said.

'I know,' Alex mumbled, her voice cracking, 'I keep sitting by the phone, waiting and waiting. We all do.'

'She might not be able to get to a phone,' Lloyd pointed out.

'What about Brody? Have you got through to her yet?' Sam asked.

I swallowed hard. Brody? There was no need to bring her and Grandad into this. I was fine!

'Nah,' Reggie said, 'nothing. I reckon her mum meant it when she said no mobiles on holiday. It's just dead when I try to text her.'

'Like Jolene might be,' Sammie said dramatically.

Everyone shouted at her to shut up.

'I'm just saying,' Sammie protested, sounding hurt.

There was a long silence. 'Well,' Reggie said finally, 'we'd best get back to After School club before Mrs Fryston sends out search parties for us, too. Unless anyone's got anything to say? Anything *constructive*.'

Nobody had but I let out this mighty sneeze. It was a good one; made them all jump ten foot into the air. Very constructive.

Chapter Eighteen

Five minutes later I was sitting in the middle of the circle, sneezing and shivering. Alex had her arms wrapped round me and so did Sammie. Reggie was pacing up and down saying, 'Flaming Nora! Under our noses all the time! Wicked!'

'She's freezing,' Sammie said, 'give her your jumpers everyone.'

'I'll do it, I'll do it!' Alex told Sammie, pushing her away as Sammie tried to tuck the sweatshirts and cardigans round my knees.

'Oh, Jolene. You are in so much trouble!' Reggie laughed.

The others told
him to belt
up but I knew
he was right.
This wasn't like
last time I'd run away at all. That was nothing
compared to this. The police were out looking
for me—Mam had been on the telly—I was in
trouble all right. Up to my neck and rising.

'Jolene, what do you want to do now?' Alex asked.

'I don't know,' I admitted. I turned to Sammie.
'Sammie, was anyone else with Mam when she
was on telly? Anyone sitting with her?'

'Er . . . yeah . . . I can't remember who they
said it was, though. He never said nothing.'

'Did he have a daft hairstyle—you know—
peroxide white and cut short?' I asked hopefully.

'No. It was grey, his hair. My mum said he
looked a bit . . .'

'A bit what?'

'Nothing.'

'A bit what?'

'A bit shifty.'

No guesses for who that was. Grandad Martin. Huh! He even managed to look shifty on television. My heart sank then. If it had been Darryl instead of Grandad Martin . . . But no, I thought, it wouldn't be, would it? *He* had enough to worry about.

'Shall I go get Mrs Fryston?' Alex asked.

'No!' I shouted. It came out louder and harsher than I meant.

'But you're shivery. You need . . .'

'No!' I repeated. 'I don't want her. I don't want anyone!'

I hugged my knees to my chest, rocking myself back and forth. One by one, they shuffled closer, keeping me warm. I looked at each of them in turn. 'Look, you lot, I know I shouldn't have come here, and I don't want to get you all done or anything but if you dob me in, I'll only run away again and this time to somewhere huge like London. That's definite, that is. All I'm asking is for you to hide me until Grandad comes back from America at the end of the month.'

Alex bit her lip and looked worried but Lloyd nodded. 'Fair enough,' he said.

'Yeah, but come on, Lloydy. Mrs Fryston will freak if she finds out,' Reggie began.

'Well, we've just got to make sure she doesn't find out then, haven't we?' Lloyd replied, his voice low and calm. I stared at him over my pile of jumpers, glad he seemed to understand. He reminded me of Keith. The sort that doesn't say much but when he does, people sit up and take notice. 'This is what I think,' Lloyd continued, 'Jolene's our friend, right?' Everyone nodded. 'Well, we should respect our friends and help them when they need help, even if it means not doing what grown-ups want us to do.'

I liked the way Lloyd thought. I couldn't have put it better myself.

'I don't know,' Reggie said, staring at me.

'What's to know?' Lloyd asked. 'Listen, you lot. Aren't you fed up with being told what to do all the time? Everywhere you go it's do this, do that, eat this, don't eat that. One minute you're too old to be playing on the swings, the next minute you're too young to be out alone in the playground. You can't even go fishing in peace without someone asking you why you're there and how old you are. There's no freedom any more. When my grandad was little he used to walk six miles to school on his own in the dark. Now kids aren't allowed to sneeze without somebody making a rule against it. Grown-ups tell us what to do all the time. What happened to letting us make our own decisions? Make our own mistakes, too, maybe, but at least they're our own mistakes.'

Like a football manager's pep-talk at half-time, Lloyd's inspirational speech did the trick. Everyone nodded and muttered things like 'He's right' and Sammie moaned her mum even asked her what she was doing when she was on the loo.

'So now what?' Reggie asked.

'Now we promise to stick together and help Jolene,' Lloyd replied. 'All in favour say "aye".'

Every one of them said 'aye', although Alex's 'aye' was a bit of a low one, but I reckoned she was still in shock at seeing me here. I couldn't blame her; I'd have been fazed too, I reckon.

'Thanks,' I whispered, giving them all a weak smile.

The mood lifted then. People began coming out with ideas about what to do and what to bring me. 'We need a password,' Reggie suggested, 'so Jolene knows it's one of us when we approach.'

Before anyone could come up with anything I sneezed again. 'There you go,' Reggie laughed, 'we'll sneeze—one for "it's us" and two for "danger".'

'And some sort of system for keeping watch. We should work in pairs, doing a stint each, so no one gets suspicious,' Lloyd said.

'What if somebody wants to use the tepee?' Sam asked.

'It's only meant to be used by the older ones anyway and seeing as we are the older ones . . .' Reggie said.

'Since when has that stopped your Ruby?' Sammie snorted.

'The girl has a point,' Reggie admitted.

'We'll have to block the entrance somehow. Or fiddle with the latch so no one can get in,' Lloyd said, immediately going towards the door and examining the keyhole. He was all fired up, this one.

'Someone should make a list of supplies and that—food and stuff,' Sammie then suggested.

'Hell, yes,' Reggie nodded, rubbing his hands together, 'we'll do all those! At last, something exciting happens at After School club. Bring it on!'

Chapter Nineteen

They left soon after, promising to be back as soon as they could. 'We'll be close by anyway, setting up the sculpture park,' Alex told me. I just nodded and pulled the beanbags up to my chin, glad I didn't have to trail round Wakefield again and could lie down in peace.

Half an hour later, the commotion started as the whole of After School club descended on the Patch. I had made myself a little nest with the beanbags close to the window and was happy just listening, working out who was where from my hiding place. There was plenty of banging and scraping and hammering. Mrs Fryston was going round each group, saying the usual things. 'That's fantastic!' 'Oh, Ruby, what a good idea!' 'Lloyd, what can I say? I love how you've angled the wheel so it catches the light. You are so talented.'

A tall shadow against the door startled me for a second until I realized it was Headless Herbert. I grinned, eager to hear what Mrs Fryston had to say about him.

'Oh, doesn't he look imposing!' she said but then added, 'Don't you think he needs to be a bit more to the side? He's blocking the door to the tepee a bit too much.'

'Oh, he looks cool just there, Mrs Fryston.'

I realized what Alex was doing then; she was using Headless Herbert as a guard to stop anyone barging in and finding me.

'Cool, yes, but I think you need to shuffle him across, just a tiny bit.'

Lloyd joined in then. 'Actually, it's perfect there, Mrs Fryston. He unifies the dynamics of the whole sculpture park. He acts as a beacon, harmonizing colour, shape, and space. To move him even a millimetre would be to destroy that fragile synchronicity.'

'Well,' Mrs Fryston said, and I could tell she didn't have a clue what he was talking about either, 'if you say so.'

She then disappeared to find another group to praise.

A few seconds later, I heard a sneeze and something dropped through the window, landing on my lap. A packet of aspirins! These guys thought of everything. I snuggled down in my  beanbags. Everything would be fine now. Everything would be mint.

I didn't leave the tepee the rest of the day. I had plenty to eat and drink from the stores the gang had brought in first thing and the aspirins had brought my temperature right down.

Next morning, I was feeling fit again, and was well perked up by the time I heard the sneezes outside and the gang trooped in. 'Mornin', Hermit,' Reggie greeted me, 'we've brought prezzies.'

'Top,' I smiled, looking round for Alex but not finding her.

'Alex isn't in yet—she's helping her mum do something,' Sammie said, as if reading my mind.

'OK,' I said, shuffling upright to check out my presents.

Reggie plonked himself down next to me. 'Right, then. Sam first.'

Sam produced a carrier bag. 'Er . . . I've brought you some stationery and pens from our shop in case you want to write letters or draw or something . . . and some breakfast bars nobody else likes at home.'

'Thanks.'

Reggie handed over a small cardboard box. 'I've brought you my Walkman to listen to. You can only borrow it, though. I want it back after. I've put loads of decent tapes in and spare batteries. How thoughtful am I?'

'Very. Thanks, Reggie.'

Sammie kneeled down in front of me, pulling

a bag from the inside of her jacket. 'Well,' she said, unrolling it, 'I noticed your hair was a right mess yesterday so I've brought you my second best hairbrush to borrow . . .' She was about to hand it over when she paused. 'You haven't got nits have you?'

'No.'

'OK then. And here's some wipes for your face and some clean knickers.' She leaned closer and whispered, though her whisper was still loud enough for everyone to hear. 'I don't mean to be embarrassin' or nothing but it's a girl thing, isn't it? Don't worry, they're brand new. I got them for my birthday but they're too small so I thought they might fit you, seeing as you're so skinny. They've got hearts on, see.'

'Er . . . great . . . yeah.'

'I've got some just the same as them,' Reggie joked, 'they fit like a glove.'

'You shouldn't even be looking!' Sammie said, stuffing the cellophane bag hurriedly away.

As each person brought my booty, the others stood watch round the door. Last up was Lloyd.

He shrugged a heavy rucksack from his back and began producing one thing after another. Torch, a compass, a blanket, a rolled-up sleeping bag, a book called *The Worst Case Scenario*—just in case, he said—small cartons of fruit juice, dried fruit, biscuits. It went on and on. 'Blimey,' I said when he'd finished, 'have you anything left at your house?'

Lloyd shrugged. 'It's only what I take when I camp out.'

'You're ace, you know that, don't you?' I told them all. 'True mates.'

Chapter Twenty

I didn't see Alex until much later. Half five, six o'clock-ish. 'Nice of you to turn up,' I joked as she sneaked in.

'I . . . I can't stay long,' she said, glancing behind her every two seconds, 'Mum and Mrs Fryston are clearing away . . . I said I'd just check the sculptures were OK.'

'Well, sit down, take a load off,' I said, pulling a spare beanbag up for her.

Alex shook her head. 'I can't. They might come looking.'

I sighed. I was feeling bored and wanted Alex

just to sit and relax with me for a second. Why did she have to be so uptight? 'OK, suit yourself,' I told her grumpily.

She began pacing up and down in front of me. 'Are you sure you want to do this, Jolene?'

'Do what?'

'Stay here hiding.'

'Course. I've got everything I need, why shouldn't I?'

'But . . . don't you want me to make a phone call to . . . to people, to let them know you're OK?'

'No, I don't.'

'Why not?'

'Because then it'll take them about two minutes to find me! I know what you're like, Alex. You're rubbish when people start asking loads of questions.'

The pacing stopped instantly. 'I'm not. I'm quite good, actually,' she said, all defensive.

'Yeah, whatever.'

She became even more grumpy and began the pacing up and down thing again which was beginning to get on my nerves. 'How will you manage until Monday?' she then asked.

'What do you mean?'

'It's Friday today . . . nearly the weekend.'

I frowned. I hadn't thought of that. Two days was a long time without visitors. 'You'll come, won't you? Sneak out for half an hour tomorrow or Sunday?'

She shook her head. 'I . . . no, I can't. We've got . . . we've got guests staying.'

Charming! Here I was, living in a blinking hut only two minutes walk from her house and she couldn't even be bothered to check how I was. After all I'd been through. 'Thanks a bunch, Alex,' I snapped. The pacing increased and I reached out my hand and grabbed her ankle to stop her. 'Pack it in, you're doing my head in!' I told her.

'Sorry,' she said, almost losing her balance but finally stopping and sitting opposite me.

Neither of us spoke for a minute. 'Please come and see me, Alex. I'll be lonely otherwise,' I said.

She shook her head. 'I can't. They'd notice if I left.'

'They'd notice if I left,' I mimicked, angry at her. Flipping heck, if it was the other way round, I'd be here every second I could, I would. Some mate she was turning out to be in an emergency.

Alex leapt to her feet then. 'I'd better go,' she said, marching towards the door.

'Yeah, you had,' I told her. 'Have a nice weekend, won't you?'

Chapter Twenty-One

As if to match my mood, it rained all weekend. I just sat huddled in Lloyd's sleeping bag, listening to it pelting down, watching the water drip. On Monday morning, the first thing Sam asked me when they all trooped in was if the tepee had leaked. 'It's been its first proper test,' he said.

'Loads, especially that part there,' I told him, pointing out the boggy patch beneath the window.

'Are you sure it's from the rain and not you?' Reggie grinned.

'Cheek! I go . . . you know . . . outside when it's dark. Over by the bush thing.'

'Oh, flipping heck! Spare me the details.'

'You asked,' I told him.

They all started talking about how I should use the loo then! 'We could bring you a bucket,' Lloyd said, 'or maybe a spade—so you can just dig a hole and cover it up again. That's probably more eco-friendly. No loo roll, though. That'd be a give-away and anyway, it's unnecessary. The Romans used to use a . . .'

Sam interrupted the history lesson. 'Hang on a minute; next year's Year Sixes have got to work in here in September. They don't want to be sitting on piles of you-know-what.'

'Do y'mind? I don't do piles! I'm not a carthorse!' I said, turning to face Alex, who had so far not said a thing. 'What about you, Alex? Any good ideas?'

'No,' she mumbled, scraping her foot across the seagrass matting. She'd better not start the pacing thing or I'd thump her.

'I didn't think you would have,' I said, still annoyed at her for not bothering to visit me at all over the weekend. It had been a long, long two days.

She stared glumly at the floor. What was with her? She'd turned into such a mardy. 'Oh, cheer up, Alex,' I told her. 'It's not like *you've* got to wee in a hole, is it?'

She glowered at me, good and proper. I was a bit taken aback, I admit it. Alex never gave me dirty looks. 'You think this is just a joke, don't you, Jolene?' she asked.

'Yeah, if you say so.'

She flung her arms round the room, pointing out all the stuff I'd got scattered about. 'And the rest of you are just as bad, running round after her like she was some lost little princess when you know people are out there, looking for her, worried sick!'

'Well, if that's how you feel, don't come any more,' Sammie told her.

'Yeah, Alex. Go get a life!' I snarled.

'Fine by me!' she said and left, just like that.

'What's eating her?' Sammie asked, handing me a toffee.

'Who cares,' I shrugged, 'I've got more important things to worry about.'

'Follow her, Lloydy,' Reggie said, 'get her to
calm down or she'll blow it.'

'OK.'

Reggie looked at Sammie and me then, shaking
his head. 'Way to go, you two. So much for
sticking together.'

'Sorry, Reg,' Sammie said instantly.

I just stared at the floor. He needn't think he
was making me feel bad about Alex. She knew
more than anyone what it was like for me with
Mam and Grandad Martin back home. Pity she
couldn't remember because, until she did, *we*
weren't talking.

Reggie moved over to the door. 'Come on, we'd
better do what we were meant to do; check out
the sculptures for rain damage. Someone'll be
over at lunch with your sandwiches later,
Jolene.'

'Right,' I said.

He stepped outside, followed by Sam and Sammie. I followed them, peering out as far as I dared. It was much sunnier today but there were still plenty of puddles where the uneven pathway dipped. I took a gulp of fresh air before Sam closed the door, an apologetic look on his face.

'Well, Headless Herbert's had it for starters,' I heard Reggie say.

'Why?' I asked, as loudly as I dared, my face pressed close to the latticed door frame.

'Half the mod rock's come unstuck and his neck's filled with water. He looks like a mummy gone wrong.'

'Oh.'

'Or a very weird bird bath.'

'Ha!' I laughed. So much for Alex's finishing him off properly.

The three of them spent a couple more minutes inspecting the sculptures. I tried tracking them, moving round inside the tepee while they moved round outside. It gave me something to do. The blind on the window rustled and a toffee dropped onto the floor. 'That's gone in the mud now!' I

 told Sammie striding across to that side.

'Soz—I forgot,' she whispered.

'No worries. Hey, if you can get me some mints next time.'

'Oh-oh.'

'What?'

'Lloyd's here and he looks . . .'

'What?'

'Hide, Jolene, hide quick!'

Chapter Twenty-Two

I scrambled beneath the beanbags and waited, my heart thumping in my chest. There was a lot of scraping around and heated whispering but I couldn't make anything out. Then the door opened and closed again quickly and Lloyd began firing instructions at me. 'Wherever you are stay hidden and don't move. As soon as you get the signal, run for it.'

I wanted to ask what signal but he was still in full flow. 'Mrs Fryston heard me talking to Alex about you outside the mobile. She asked what was going on and I said nothing but Alex burst out crying. I've got the feeling she'll crack.'

Yeah, I thought, clenching my fist, me too.

Lloyd didn't speak again but seemed to be shifting things round all over the place. It was the same outside; what were they doing? Reorganizing the whole of the sculpture park? The answer to that must have been yes because a few seconds later I heard Mrs Fryston's voice, asking Reggie to move this and that back to where it came from. She didn't sound angry or anything. At first.

'Don't you think the stuff looks better like this, Mrs F? All clustered together? We do, don't we, guys?'

'Yeah, we do,' Sammie and Sam chorused.

'Move it all away from the door, please.'

'Can't, Mrs F. Especially Herbert. He's undergoing emergency repairs.'

'Well, do the repair job over there, Reggie. I want to look inside the tepee.'

'Can't shift him. The water's weighed him down . . .'

There was a loud scraping and I heard Sammie gasp and Reggie go, 'Blooming heck, Mrs Fryston, have you been going to the gym?'

I had to begin my breathing exercises then, because I knew she was on her way in and I knew she knew what she was going to find. The latch clicked and I sensed her stepping inside. 'Ah, Lloyd,' Mrs Fryston said, her tone not quite as patient by now.

'Hi,' Lloyd replied.

'Would you mind standing up, please. I'd like to check beneath that heap of things you've got stacked up there.'

'Why?'

'Just move please, Lloyd.'

'Nah! I'm happy here, thanks.'

'Well, I'm far from happy that you're here. You should be over in the mobile, like I asked.'

'Happy here.'

Mrs Fryston took a deep breath then, as if to gather all her patience together. 'Lloyd, I need you to move,' she said in a firm voice.

I was so busy listening to Lloyd and Mrs Fryston that I didn't feel the tug on my beanbag at first. Then it came again. And again. Followed by a kick. Mrs Fryston wasn't the only one wanting someone to move. I got it then: the signal. Lloyd's pile was the decoy, giving me a chance to escape. Slowly, like a tortoise reversing, I began to back out, edging bit by bit along the walls of the tepee. I made it as far as the door and even managed to get to the outside. It was when I tried to stand up and run for it I came unstuck. I was squinting so much in the daylight that I tripped straight over Herbert's metal base which sent me flying onto the gravel. By the time I was on my feet, Mrs Fryston had her arms round my shoulders and as much as I tried to twist and turn, I could not escape from her grasp. 'Get off me,' I kept yelling, 'you aren't allowed to touch me!'

'No you're not,' Lloyd said, standing in front of us and looking angrily at her.

Mrs Fryston just gripped me closer and began bellowing at him at the top of her lungs. 'Be quiet, Lloyd! And that goes for all of you! You are all in enough trouble as it is! Now get over to that mobile. This instant!'

I was used to teachers shouting at me but even I jumped then. It was more scary, somehow, coming from Mrs Fryston, who never lost her temper. The effect on the others was immediate. Sammie and Sam both went bright red and looked nervously at each other and even Reggie couldn't think of a comeback this time. Instead he walked over to Lloyd and nudged him. 'Come on, mate. Let's go.'

Lloyd's eyes watered and he glanced at me. 'Sorry, Jolene,' he said.

'Don't worry about it,' I told him, 'it's Alex that'll be sorry.'

Chapter Twenty-Three

The funniest bit that happened next was when Mrs Fryston marched us into the mobile and everybody in there carried on as normal. Brandon even came up to me and said, 'Oh, hello, Jolene, want to play sharks?'

Mrs Fryston told him 'Not right now, Brandon,' and made him go to one of the playleaders. She then clapped her hands and announced that she wanted everyone to go outside and get some fresh air before lunch. The playleaders, noticing me for the first time, quickly started shepherding the kids into the playground. Alex, I realized, was not among them and nor was Mrs McCormack. Coward, I thought. Running home with Mummy.

As soon as the last kid had left I expected Mrs Fryston to start blasting us all again but instead she reached out and began checking my hands. 'That was a nasty fall,' she said, looking at the grit and scraped skin on my palms. She told Sammie to fetch the first aid box. 'Are you OK, Jolene?' Mrs Fryston asked.

I shrugged. 'It's only a few scratches. I get worse playing football in the park.'

'No, I mean, are you OK? You're not hurt? Or injured? From anything that's happened to you in the past week?'

I shook my head and she let out a sigh of relief. 'Thank goodness for that.' Sammie brought the first aid box and Mrs Fryston began to clean my hands, all the time asking us questions in her old, calm manner.

Nobody tried to fib. There was no point. In the end, Mrs Fryston shook her head. 'Well, I wondered why the tepee had gone from "flavour of the month" one minute to "a boring dump" the next and now I know. I can't believe I never cottoned on. Oh, what a mess.'

'Are we in big trouble, Mrs Fryston?' Sammie asked. Her bottom lip was going; the waterworks would start any second. I knew from last summer this girl could fill dams.

Mrs Fryston gave her a little smile but didn't deny it. 'Well, I will have to call the police soon and they will want to talk to all of you. And I have to warn you they won't treat what you did as a game, Sammie.'

'Good, because it wasn't a game! We were helping a friend,' Lloyd said, his whole body tense. The lad was still pumped up and I felt glad I had one fighter still left on the team. That would come in useful. Now that I'd got over being discovered, I was planning my next move.

Mrs Fryston gave Sammie the first aid box to put back and told her to go wash her face, sending Sam with her for company, before she replied to Lloyd. Her voice was warm and sympathetic. 'I'm sorry, Lloyd. I didn't mean to patronize you. I know it wasn't a game to you, and I admire your loyalty, but you have to see all sides. The police have spent hours searching the city for Jolene.'

'So? That's their job! At least she's alive, so that's a result, right?'

Mrs Fryston's face was a picture then! She looked so shocked because Lloyd wasn't being a good little boy and backing down but I don't know why she should have been. I mean, the kid was home-schooled. His parents encouraged him to be independent. He camped out; he used a knife to gut fish he'd caught by himself. He wasn't a follower like the others. Like Alex. Oh, my blood boiled when I thought of her. What a wimp she'd turned out to be. What a snitch. The sparks started in my head the more I thought about her. But the sparks were bad news; they made me lash out and do stupid things. I had to stay focused. Five currant buns. Five currant buns in a baker's shop . . .

'Jolene? Jolene?' Mrs Fryston repeated, touching my arm.

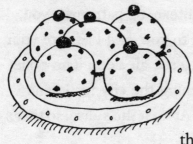 'Sorry, miles away, miss,' I said and gave her a little, feeble smile. I had to keep it polite. Make her think I was just going to sit here and wait for the police to lecture me and send me back to Mam.

'I asked why, Jolene. Why did you run away?'

I just shrugged and stared at the floor. 'I don't know, miss. I was just being silly, I suppose.'

I don't think she knew what to say to that. Instead she told us all to sit down for a minute and she reached into her handbag and took out her mobile. Reggie perked up then. 'I'm innocent! I demand to see my lawyer!' he joked, thinking, like we all did, she was calling the police. Mrs Fryston held her hand up for him to be quiet and started talking into her phone. Reggie plonked himself down, looking deflated.

'Andrew?' Mrs Fryston said. 'Are you still in your office? Brilliant! Can you come across to the mobile, please . . . something's cropped up.'

That's handy, isn't it? Being married to the headteacher of the school, especially one who spends his summer holidays sorting out paper-work. Andrew—Mr Sharkey—was over before you could say 'busted'. It was going to be harder to do a runner now, that was for sure.

While the missus brought him up to speed with the good news, I glanced round. I was about ten strides away from the door, that was all, but I could see Sammie standing on the other side of it, dabbing her eyes and talking to Sam. The pair of them were blocking my exit. Well, tough. They'd just have to shift or get trampled on, wouldn't they? I rose slowly from my seat. If anybody asked, I was going to the bogs.

I managed one step before I felt a hand on my shoulder. 'Jolene, I want you to come somewhere with me,' Mrs Fryston said.

Bogger, I thought. Bogger, bogger, bogger.

'Jan, I think you're making a mistake. You should wait until the police get here,' Mr Sharkey told her, frowning at me.

She waved a set of car keys at him. 'I know, I

know, but I think it's important to do this first.
Give me five minutes.'

'Jan!'

'Five minutes.'

Chapter Twenty-Four

It took only two of the five minutes to get to Alex's house.

'What are we doing here?' I asked, scowling as Mrs Fryston levered me out of the back of her car.

'There's something here I think you should see. Or someone,' she said, pressing the doorbell.

I began struggling then, trying to free myself. 'If you think I'm apologizing to that tell-tale, you've got another think coming. In fact, I wouldn't even let me go in there, if I were you.'

'Well, it's a risk I'm willing to take,' Mrs Fryston

said gripping me firmly. Reggie was right, I reckoned; she had been going to the gym.

Mrs McCormack opened the door and her hand flew to her mouth when she saw me. 'Oh, Jolene,' she said and she had the same catch in her voice as Mrs Fryston had when she'd cleaned my scratches. Like she really cared I was OK. Not that I cared that she cared. Not one bit.

'Y'all reet, Mrs McCormack?' I mumbled.

'Are they still here?' Mrs Fryston asked her, pulling me with her into the house.

'Yes,' Mrs McCormack replied, 'we were just getting ready to come to you.'

I was concentrating too hard on not losing focus to work out what they were talking about. This wasn't the nice house where I'd had good times in the past, I kept telling myself. Being here was like being among Toon supporters at St James's Park as far as I was concerned—deep into enemy territory. Mrs Fryston stopped at the hat stand and turned to smile at me. 'Go with Ann, Jolene, but you haven't got long. I do have to take you back in a minute.'

'Whatever,' I muttered, following Mrs McCormack towards the living room.

I had hardly stepped through the doorway when I heard screams, followed by the thunder of feet, and before I had time to catch my breath, I was being whirled in the air by a big bloke with a bristly chin. While he was doing that, two lads were pulling at my legs, yelling and shouting.

'Jolene! Jolene! Thank God!' Darryl cried.

'Put her down! We want to hold her!' Jack protested.

Darryl did as he was told, plonking me down on the carpet, and next thing I knew I was being smothered by Jack and Keith. My brain kept throwing out little words like 'what?' and 'but!' and 'how?' but I never managed to say any of them.

The next part was all a bit of a blur, to be honest. Darryl was talking so fast and I was still dazed from the speed of everything since being found, it was hard to take everything in at once.

I'll tell you what I remember Darryl telling me. Darryl and the lads had been staying at Alex's since last Friday—they were who those guests had been. It turned out he had found out Alex's family's number from Directory Enquiries and been calling them since the police suspected I was in the area, just in case the McCormacks heard anything. Apparently my mam wouldn't talk to Darryl; she'd been telling everyone it was his fault I had run off in the first place so he had no right to know anything from her. Anyway, Darryl mentioned to Mrs McCormack how the lads were convinced I was hiding in the Yorkshire Sculpture Park we'd visited and how desperate they were to have a look for themselves. 'The police don't know the good hiding places,' Jack had kept saying. In the end, because she thought it might help, Mrs McCormack had suggested they come up for the weekend. 'We spent all day Saturday and all day Sunday searching, didn't we, lads?'

Jack and Keith nodded, their heads bobbing like seals in water.

'We got absolutely drenched on both days. We

should have gone back yesterday but Jacko here came down with a temperature, didn't you? We had a right night with him, daft lad.'

'I'm better now!' Jack cried as he clung to me, but when I looked at him properly, I could see that his face was pasty and he looked washed out. But then so did Keith and so did Darryl. It hit me, then, why Alex had been in a mardy with me. I glanced round, seeing her for the first time standing by the mantelpiece, watching us all. Her eyes were red from crying.

'Did you go to the Sculpture Park too?' I asked her.

She just nodded and wiped her eyes with the back of her sleeve. 'Both days,' she said.

'I'm sorry, Alex,' I told her, my voice cracking, 'I never thought anyone would come looking for me. I thought nobody cared.'

'Well, you got that wrong!' she said.

'Well wrong!' Keith added.

'I know,' I said, patting him but looking directly at Alex and feeling totally ashamed of myself for the things I'd called my best mate. 'I was out of order—you know—in the tepee. I wish I could undo everything—cast a spell or something to go back in time.'

'Like Tinkerbell can,' Jack whispered.

Alex just nodded. 'I know,' she said.

'We all wish that, hinny,' Darryl said. 'I don't know how many times I've wished I could turn the clock back and not say what I said to you at work that day.'

'Honest?' I asked.

His face tightened. 'It makes me shudder every time I think about it. You caught me at a really bad time, Jolene. I'd just been told by the solicitors if I didn't find a place soon, Tracie could get the lads living with her full time and he'd told me as far as you were concerned I had no chance because you weren't my biological daughter. Oh, I was in such a state. "But I love her like she's my own," I said, "and the lads love her like a sister." Then when you came flying in, so full of beans . . . oh, I didn't know what to say for the best and I got it totally wrong, like the idiot I am.'

I just stared when he said that. All right, I cried.

Cried more than Sammie Waterworks Wesley, if you must know. We all did.

'Hey,' Darryl said, wiping the tears on my face with his thumb and making me laugh, 'the good news is we've got a council flat in Lamesley. We move in at the end of August. How about that, then?'

'That's mint.'

'You can see the Angel of the North outside your bedroom window!' Keith said.

'My bedroom window?'

'For when you come and stay,' Darryl smiled.

Mrs Fryston knocked on the door and interrupted then, which is a good job otherwise Mrs McCormack's living room would have been flooded. 'I'm sorry, everybody, but it's time to call Jolene's mum now and the police. We have to go.'

I didn't argue. Whatever happened next didn't matter now. I knew Darryl and the lads loved me and Alex was my friend again and that was all that counted.

Epilogue

If you're expecting me to go into loads of details about what happened next, I can't. I can tell you some of it, just to wind everything up properly, like, but if you want the real nitty-gritty you'll have to ask someone else. Sorry and all that but I'm stressed out because school starts tomorrow and I haven't got half my stuff ready *and* I've got to see counsellor-lady again after my little adventure. So much for a fresh start at secondary school but, like Mam said, what did I expect when my face had been plastered all over the local papers? Counsellor-lady needn't be thinking she's getting more cakes out of me, that's all I can say.

I suppose giving you a run-down isn't such a bad idea. It'll be good preparation in case I have to write about what I did in the holidays. As if I'm telling!

I'll kick off with the police thing. Now *that* was a right hoo-ha. They asked me thousands of questions, searched the tepee, told me that no matter how bad things seemed at home, running away was never the answer, and that if I ever had problems again I should phone the *Childline* number. I told them not to worry, because running away is ninety-nine per cent boring anyway and I had no plans to repeat the exercise. They said that was good to hear because next time I might not be so lucky and, though I hate to admit it, I know they're right.

Reggie, Sammie, Sam, and Lloyd got a lecture too, about how they might have *thought* they were doing the right thing but in fact they weren't actually helping matters at all. I wasn't there when they got their talking to, otherwise I'd have complained because I didn't see why they should get done because of me. Apparently everyone was petrified apart from Lloyd who kept making a point about how we were all free to make our own choices, even if we were only ten or eleven years old, whether it inconvenienced authority or not. If you ask me, Lloyd Fountain's going to be famous one day. Or prime minister—one or the other.

Then, of course, there was Mam. She arrived with Grandad Martin later that evening and everything happened just exactly like I told you it would. She was all over me like a rash at first, kissing me and sobbing buckets and showing me my Sunderland shirt that she'd kept under her pillow every night. It was in a terrible state—all smudged from where her mascara had rubbed off. Honestly. She told the police—not for the first time, by the sound of it—that I'd run away because her ex-husband had been heartless and dumped me just like he'd dumped her. When I said, well, it wasn't just that, was it, what about you going on the cruise ships and making me change schools, she gave one of her fake laughs and said, 'Oh, Jolene. I was never serious about that, you silly thing.'

As soon as we got in the car she had a go at me for showing her up. 'Here's me just happy to see my baby alive and what happens? She makes up lies about me.' Course Grumpy Grandad Martin stuck his oar in then and said what did she expect? I'd always been a bad 'un, right from the start. I told him to put a sock in it and he told me if I didn't watch out I'd end up in care. I told him I'd rather be put in care with Dracula than live with him and Nana so he stopped the car on the hard shoulder of the motorway and would have given me a right back hander if Mam hadn't stopped him. That was a first, her sticking up for me.

To be fair, she's been a lot better with me since I came back. I think it really did frighten her when I ran away this time and she was upset when I'd made it so obvious I preferred Darryl to her. 'Broke my heart, that did,' she kept telling me. I suppose I had been a bit harsh on her but, like when I first heard about her and Darryl splitting up and I wasn't very sympathetic, when you've been let down by someone as often as I have, that's just how it is. You kind of stop feeling anything for the person. And it's not as if she's turned into a sweet as apple pie mam since, either. Don't worry, she still loses it and cracks me one when I wind her up but it's not as often. She's way less stressed now there's just the two of us and Grandad Jake gave her some money for bills.

What else. Oh, Darryl and the lads, of course. Well, in the beginning Mam still had the hump with Darryl so when he phoned the first few times to check out how I was and if he could take me to the footy, she just hung up on him. Then Mandy and Risa came back on the scene because their cruise had been cancelled due to food poisoning and she wanted to go on all-nighters with them. Mam daren't leave me alone in case I ran off again and Grandad Martin refused to have me (ooh, I was so gutted, I was) so she let Darryl stay over and look after me a couple of weekends and then when he moved into his new flat, I stayed over there. I stay most weekends now. The new place needs a bit of work but Darryl will soon have it sorted. Keith's already filled his side of the bedroom with car posters and Jack's filled his side with Peter Pan ones. We're just waiting for my Sunderland AFC wallpaper to arrive then we can get started on mine. You know, I hope Lloyd does become prime minister because then he can change the law so that top blokes like Darryl get the same rights as real dads if they split up from your mam. It's not fair otherwise, is it?

What else, what else? Nothing really. I don't hear much from Alex now, though she did invite me to the end of the holidays party they had at After School club. I told her I couldn't go because it was too far to come but really I didn't fancy it. If I'm honest, it hasn't been the same with Alex since that last time I saw her at her house, even though I said sorry and everything. I've talked to Brody about it and she says it's like when you break a favourite pot and glue it back again. It kind of looks the same but it's never quite right. Brody told me I missed a fun party though. Because so many people were leaving—her, Reggie, Sammie, and Sam—Mrs Fryston really pushed the boat out and hired a disco and everything. I hadn't realized all four of them were leaving—I'd have sent them something if I had— but it figures. Sam and Sammie are like me, in Year Seven next, and Brody and Reggie are Year Eight. I can't see me going back to that After School club again, either. You have to move on, don't you?

The times I do feel close to Alex are when I'm staying over at Darryl's and I look out of my bedroom window. Keith was spot-on, you can see the Angel of the North—just—if you stand on a chair and use binoculars. It's not the Angel I see, though, it's Headless Herbert, and when I think of him I think of that afternoon I spent with Alex, laughing so much it hurt.

Oh well, haway then, and get your lip gloss on.

Jolene Nevin-Birtley